Christmas is a time for giving

Gifts are not always things you can
hold in your hands. The gift we celebrate
at Christmas is that small baby born in a
stable, though the shepherds and the wise men
did manage to bring presents as well.

These books also celebrate Christmas,
and each deals with a different gift,
the kind that can bring immeasurable love
and contentment down the years—
which we wish for all of you.

Enjoy!

GW00727919

Jennifer Taylor has been writing Mills & Boon®
romances for some time, but only recently 'discovered'
Medical Romances™. She was so captivated by these
heart-warming stories that she immediately set out to
write them herself! As a former librarian who worked
in scientific and industrial research, Jennifer enjoys the
research involved with the writing of each book as well
as the chance it gives her to create a cast of wonderful
new characters. When not writing or doing research for
her latest book, Jennifer's hobbies include reading,
travel, and walking her dog. She lives in the north-west
of England with her husband and children.

Recent titles by the same author:

FOR BEN'S SAKE*
GREATER THAN RICHES
TENDER LOVING CARE
THE HUSBAND SHE NEEDS**

Dalverston General Hospital
** A Country Practice*

A REAL FAMILY CHRISTMAS

BY
JENNIFER TAYLOR

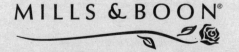

First published in Great Britain 2000
Harlequin Mills & Boon Limited,
Eton House, 18-24 Paradise Road, Richmond, Surrey TW9 1SR

© Jennifer Taylor 2000

ISBN 0 263 82277 X

Set in Times Roman 10½ on 11¼ pt.
03-1200-56244

Printed and bound in Spain
by Litografia Rosés, S.A., Barcelona

CHAPTER ONE

'I KNOW what I'm going to ask Santa for!'

Emma Graham, staff nurse on the Obs and Gynae Ward of St Luke's Hospital, put down her coffee-cup and looked expectantly at her friend, Linda Wood. It was two weeks before Christmas and the canteen where they were having their morning break was strewn with garishly coloured tinsel and baubles.

The whole hospital seemed to be gearing itself up for the festivities, in fact. There was much talk of Christmas parties and family visits, shopping and suchlike. Emma had remained aloof from it all as her situation was rather different to that of her friends. With no family of her own, Christmas Day was usually spent by herself if she wasn't working. It was rarely a time for celebration. However, she was as eager as everyone else was to hear what the irrepressible Linda had to say so she prompted her friend to continue.

'What? I can see you're dying to tell us, Linda, so what would you like to find in your Christmas stocking this year, then?'

'Daniel Hutton!' Linda's face broke into a mischievous grin. 'I mean, come on, girls, who wouldn't want to wake up on Christmas morning and find dishy Daniel at the bottom of your bed?'

'I'd rather find him in it, thank you. Then I'd really believe in Father Christmas!'

Everyone roared with laughter as Eileen Pierce, the oldest member of staff on their ward, added her own pithy comments. Emma joined in, although she couldn't help feeling a bit uncomfortable. Daniel Hutton was sitting at a table not far from where they were sitting and he could have overheard what they'd said.

She glanced round and felt her face heat when she found that he was looking their way. His hazel eyes held a hint of amusement as they met hers before he stood up. Gathering together the papers he'd been reading, he left the canteen without a backward glance.

'I think he heard you,' Emma said with a grimace, turning back to her friend.

'Did he? Good. Maybe it will make him get his act together.' Linda wasn't in the least abashed. 'I mean, it isn't *normal* for a man who looks like he does to pay such little attention to the opposite sex! And before anyone states the obvious, I have it on good authority that Daniel showed a healthy interest in the female of the species before he came to work here. An *extremely* healthy interest, according to my friend Sonia, who worked with him!'

'Hmmm, curiouser and curiouser. I wonder what happened? Do you think it was a relationship that went sour and put him off women?' Jane Goodyear, their second-year student, looked thoughtful as she stared at the door through which Daniel had disappeared.

'Could be.' Linda chuckled. 'Maybe he needs counselling. Now, there's a thought!'

Emma shook her head in despair. 'I thought you were crazy about your Gary? Didn't you say that you were getting engaged this Christmas?'

'So? Just because I'll soon have a ring on my finger doesn't mean that I have to give up *all* life's little pleasures!'

There was a lot of laughter as they finished their break and went back to the ward. It was busy as usual, with two new cases having been admitted that morning. However, several times Emma found her thoughts straying to Daniel Hutton.

He had started work at St Luke's in the summer and there

had been a lot of speculation about the handsome senior registrar ever since. The fact that Daniel had kept himself very much to himself for the past six months had only heightened the interest in him. Nobody knew much about him, apart from the fact that he was good at his job and marvellous with the patients who came under his care.

Emma couldn't help wondering if Jane had been right about him having been put off women because of a relationship that had gone wrong. It seemed the most logical explanation. With those classically handsome looks and lean, six-foot frame, Daniel wouldn't have had a problem persuading any number of willing volunteers to go out with him!

'Can you get Mrs Horrocks ready to go down to Theatre, please, Staff?' Sister Carter popped her head round the office door as she spied Emma passing. 'Dr Hutton phoned to say that he would be up in a few minutes to have a word with her about her operation.'

'Certainly, Sister.' Emma replied. 'I was just going to check how Mrs Rogers is doing. It's the first time she's tried taking a shower on her own.'

'Fine. Do that first and then sort out Mrs Horrocks. And try to calm her down, will you?' Sister Carter rolled her eyes. 'I've never seen anyone worry as much as that poor woman does!'

Emma laughed. 'I know! The night staff said that she'd hardly slept a wink.'

'Why doesn't that surprise me? Still, she should get a bit of a nap once they give her the anaesthetic.'

Emma laughed as Sister Carter went back to her paperwork. Despite being a martinet when it came to work, the ward sister had a particularly droll sense of humour and Emma enjoyed working with her. She tapped on the bathroom door then went in to see how Mrs Rogers was faring. She found her sitting on a stool, looking extremely shaky.

'Not feeling so good, Mrs Rogers?' Emma asked solicitously as she went to help her.

'Just a bit giddy in the head, that's all,' Shirley Rogers
replied, summoning a smile.

It was so typical of her, Emma thought as she helped the
woman into her dressing-gown and took her back to the
ward. Shirley Rogers had been admitted for a total hysterectomy to remove a severely prolapsed uterus. The operation had gone very well but it had still been a major one.
However, despite being in some discomfort, Shirley hadn't
complained once.

She was a farmer's wife with three strapping sons who
all worked on the family farm. Emma knew that Shirley's
main concern was that she would be well enough to return
home for Christmas. However, she made a note to mention
to Shirley's husband that he must make sure his wife didn't
do too much when she returned home. Shirley needed a
few weeks' rest to get over the operation before she started
rushing around.

Once Shirley Rogers was comfortably settled, Emma
went to Mrs Horrocks's bed. She was just about to draw
the curtains around it when Daniel Hutton arrived.

'Thanks.' He treated her to one of his wonderful and far
too rare smiles as she paused to let him pass, and Emma
felt her heart suddenly knock against her ribs in the most
peculiar fashion. A touch of colour warmed her cheeks and
she saw one of his elegant brows rise as though he was
wondering what had caused her to blush like that.

'You're welcome.' She swished the curtains around the
bed and took a deep breath. She hadn't believed herself
susceptible to Daniel Hutton's undoubted charms but
maybe she had been a bit over-confident! However, all it
took was the sight of Jean Horrocks's woebegone face to
focus her mind firmly on work once again. The poor
woman was obviously scared stiff by the thought of the

operation she was about to undergo and Emma's tender heart went out to her.

'Now, come along, Mrs Horrocks, there's no need to worry.' Emma patted the woman's hand. 'It really is a very simple operation, as Dr Hutton will explain.'

Emma looked expectantly at Daniel who, on cue, began to add his reassurances. Carefully, he explained what would happen when Jean Horrocks went down to Theatre, taking her through each step of the procedure. Mrs Horrocks had suffered for a number of years from menorrhagia, prolonged and heavy menstrual bleeding. She was to undergo a dilatation and curettage that day, commonly referred to as a D and C.

It was a simple operation which involved removing the thickened lining of the uterus under general anaesthetic. Although there were other means of removing the endometrium, the lining of the womb, their consultant, Max Dennison, was of the old school and still preferred a D and C over more modern methods.

'So you see, Mrs Horrocks, it's all very simple, as Staff Nurse Graham told you it was.' Daniel treated the woman to his wonderful smile as he came to the end of his explanation. Emma barely managed to conceal her amazement when the older woman smiled back.

'I understand that now you've explained it to me, Dr Hutton.' Jean Horrocks settled back against the pillows, a distinctly coquettish smile curving her lips. 'I won't worry any more now that I know I'm in your capable hands.'

'I'm pleased to hear it.' One last megawatt smile then Daniel turned to Emma. 'Mrs Horrocks is scheduled for twelve o'clock, I believe, Staff. If you would page me when she leaves the ward I'll make sure I'm there to meet her when she arrives at Theatre.'

'Of course, Doctor,' Emma replied smoothly, hiding a grin as he treated her to a conspiratorial wink under cover of leaving. Obviously, Daniel had no qualms about laying on the charm if it meant that he wouldn't have an agitated and possibly disruptive patient arriving at Theatre to deal with!

'Ooh, isn't he lovely? So understanding as well. I just wish that I'd seen him when I first arrived instead of that other doctor…what was his name now?'

'Mr Dennison,' Emma supplied helpfully, checking the tags on Mrs Horrocks's wrist and ankle. They both matched, giving details of her name, date of birth and the operation she was scheduled for, so Emma initialled the notes which would accompany the patient to Theatre, confirming that the check had been done.

'That's right…Dennison.' Mrs Horrocks sniffed. 'I didn't take to him, to be honest. Told me that there was nothing to fuss about. Well, it might be nothing to him because he's a man, but it's something to me. It's my insides they're playing around with when all's said and done!'

'Which is why Dr Hutton will take such good care of you,' Emma soothed as she heard the panic creeping into Mrs Horrocks's voice once more. It seemed to do the trick because the woman relaxed again.

'Of course he will.'

Mercifully, the porters arrived at that moment to take her down to Theatre. Emma only just managed to contain her amusement as Mrs Horrocks waved to the rest of the patients as she was wheeled out of the ward. Linda stopped what she was doing and stared, open-mouthed, after the departing trolley.

'Are my eyes deceiving me or was that really Jean Horrocks on her way for her op?'

'Nope, there's nothing wrong with your eyesight.' Emma laughed ruefully. 'Hard to believe it's the same woman who's been worrying herself into an early grave for the past twenty-four hours, isn't it?'

'What did you do to her? Give her laughing gas or something?' Linda demanded.

'Something far more effective than that—ten minutes of quality time with our Dr Hutton, Emma explained. 'Worked wonders, hasn't it?'

'Too right it has! Mind you, ten minutes of dishy Daniel's time would work wonders for me, too!' Linda rolled her eyes lasciviously. Emma knew that Linda was joking but she couldn't help feeling a little irritated at her friend's insistence on calling Daniel Hutton by that ridiculous name. However, it seemed wiser not to say anything so she passed it off and carried on with her work.

There was always plenty to be done, with patients coming and going to Theatre plus the ones who were in for observation or tests. Emma had been on the ward for almost a year now and she loved her job. There was always something different to deal with.

The ward was divided into two by folding screens which were rarely closed. One side was for gynae cases and the other for obstetric patients. The only time she felt a bit down about her work was when they had a patient who had suffered a miscarriage. It was always hard to be comforting and give hope when a much-wanted baby had been lost.

They had admitted such a case that morning, a young woman in her early twenties who had miscarried the previous evening. Her name was Alison Banks and she was going to need a D and C as part of the placenta had been retained inside her womb. She was still in a state of shock so Emma had made a point of checking on her as often as she could. When she went to the bed, she found Alison crying.

'Are you OK?' she asked softly, drawing the curtain closed behind her before she approached the bed. Alison's husband was in the army and had been sent on a peace-keeping mission a month earlier. With no other family in the area to turn to, Alison was very much on her own.

'Yes. No. I don't know how I feel…' Alison ran a hand over her face and sighed. 'I keep wondering why it happened. Was it something I did? Was there something wrong with the baby? My head is spinning with it all.'

'Has Dr Hutton seen you?' Emma asked quietly, passing her a tissue.

'Yes.' Alison blew her nose but tears were still welling in her eyes.

'And what did he say?' Emma prompted. Sometimes the only way to help was to make a woman talk about what had happened.

'That it was just something that wasn't meant to be. He said that it wasn't anything I'd done and that I wasn't to blame myself. He wouldn't have told me that if it wasn't true, would he?' Alison looked beseechingly at her and Emma shook her head.

'No, he wouldn't. Dr Hutton has told you the truth, Alison. I know how hard it must be but you mustn't blame yourself.'

Emma stayed a few minutes longer then left when she was sure that Alison was a little calmer. Sister had contacted Alison's husband's regiment so that they could pass a message to him. Emma wasn't sure if he would be allowed to return home but she was hoping that he would be. Alison needed him here beside her at a time like this.

The day flew past. Before she knew it, it was time to go home. Linda offered her a lift but Emma regretfully refused. She was a bit like Old Mother Hubbard, she thought as she left the hospital, because her cupboards were completely bare! It was definitely time to visit the supermarket and stock up on essentials.

The town centre was bustling when she stepped off the bus. There was late-night shopping, with it being the run-up to Christmas, and it looked as though most of Clearsea's inhabitants had decided to make the most of the opportunity.

Emma got caught up in a crowd coming out of the chemist's and had to fight free of the crush. People were laden down with parcels and boxes, even Christmas trees. She couldn't help feeling a little left out as she felt the buzz that was in the air that night. She wasn't rostered to work that Christmas Day and she couldn't help thinking how lonely it was going to be in her flat all by herself…

'Oof!' Emma gasped as someone cannoned into her. She put out a steadying hand and just saved the little girl from a nasty fall as the child teetered on the edge of the pavement.

'That was quite a bump, wasn't it?' she said, bending down to smile at the child. She looked to be about six years old, with long dark curls and heavily lashed hazel eyes. Funnily enough, the child reminded her of someone she knew, although for the life of her Emma couldn't think who it was.

'I'm sorry.' The child looked uncertainly at her then shot a glance at the crowd milling around them. Emma looked up as well, expecting to see an anxious mother or father rushing towards them. However, nobody seemed to be taking any notice of them. It made her wonder where the little girl's parents could be. Surely she hadn't been allowed to come shopping on her own on a busy night like this?

'Isn't there anyone with you?' she asked the child, taking hold of her hand as they were jostled about.

'Uncle Daniel. We're doing our Christmas shopping tonight 'cos it will be too busy on Saturday, you see.' Two fat tears started to slither down the child's cheeks as she stared at the crowd of people. 'I was holding his hand and then this lady pushed me and now I can't see him!'

'Shh! It's all right, poppet. Don't cry. I'm sure your Uncle Daniel will be here in a moment.' Emma picked up the child. It was so busy that she was afraid that the little girl would get trampled in the crush. Where on earth was her uncle? she thought angrily. And why hadn't he had the sense to keep tight hold of his niece's hand?

'There he is! Over there! See. Uncle Daniel…Uncle Daniel!' The child's shout of joy made Emma smile. She turned to look where the little girl was pointing and was completely taken aback to see Daniel Hutton hurriedly making his way towards them.

His face broke into a relieved smile as he lifted the little girl out of Emma's arms. 'Thank heavens for that! I was having kittens when you disappeared like that, you little horror!'

The little girl chuckled. 'You can't have kittens, Uncle Daniel. Only mummy cats have kittens!'

'Well, it felt like it!' Daniel's tone was rueful but there was no doubting that he had been extremely worried. He turned to Emma and smiled gratefully at her. 'I don't know how to thank you. One minute I had hold of Amy's hand and the next she'd disappeared. I must have aged ten years in the past few minutes when I couldn't find her!'

'I can imagine!' Emma laughed softly, not finding it in her heart to scold him for having let go of his niece when it was obvious that it had been an accident and not carelessness.

She pushed back a strand of her short blond hair with a gloved hand as she searched for something to say. Although Daniel was never less than courteous whenever he visited the ward, she hadn't held a conversation with him in the whole six months he'd been at St Luke's. She wasn't sure whether she should just say goodbye or swop a few pleasantries first.

She decided that the first option would be best. 'Well, I'd better let you—'

'Would you like a cup—?'

They both spoke together then stopped. Daniel smiled; his hazel eyes were full of amusement as he looked at her.

'Snap! Anyway, you go first. Mine wasn't anything important.'

Emma hesitated, wishing that she knew what he'd been going to say. Had he been about to invite her for a cup of coffee, perhaps? She sighed, realising that she might have missed her chance now. Funnily enough, she would have welcomed the opportunity to get to know him better, she realised.

'I was just going to say that I'd better not keep you. Amy—is it?' She carried on when Daniel nodded. 'Amy told me that you'd brought her into town to do some Christmas shopping.'

'That's right, although I'm beginning to regret it. I never imagined it would be such a scrum!' His tone was so wry that Emma laughed.

'I'm afraid it tends to get like this round Christmas time. Anyway, so long as Amy is all right I'd better be off.' She edged away, half hoping that he would stop her. She quickened her pace as it struck her how foolish that was. Why should Daniel want to detain her now that he had his niece back safe and sound?

'Emma, hold on a second!'

She stopped as she heard him calling her. It took a moment for him to reach her and she couldn't help noticing how uncomfortable he looked. It made her wonder what on earth he wanted to say to her. Well, there was one easy way to find out!

'Yes?'

'I…um, well, I…er…just wanted to ask you something,' he stumbled in obvious embarrassment.

It was so out of character for him to behave that way that Emma gaped at him. Daniel had exuded an aura of calm professionalism whenever she'd had occasion to speak to him in the past, although the conversation had always centred on work before. Obviously, he wanted to ask her something of a personal nature now and her heart leapt as she tried to work out what it might be.

'Yes?' she prompted, her mind racing. Was…was Daniel about to ask her out on a date perhaps? It was a tantalising idea, even though she had never thought about him in that context before. Oh, she'd been aware of Daniel ever since he had started work at St. Luke's—who hadn't? But when had her interest shifted from objective to subjective?

'Have you ever had the feeling that you could be making a complete idiot of yourself?' His tone was rueful now. Emma laughed softly and—she hoped—encouragingly.

'Frequently! But I try not to let it deter me. Look, Daniel, if there's something you want to ask me then just fire away. I promise you that I don't bite!'

'All right, then.' He took a deep breath then rushed on. 'Can you sew, Emma?'

CHAPTER TWO

'PARDON? D-did you say what I think you did?' Emma stared at Daniel in confusion and saw him grimace.

'Yes. Look, I knew it was a bad idea. Forget I said anything, will you?'

He turned to leave, his face a mixture of embarrassment and chagrin. However, there was no way that Emma could let him go without finding out why he had asked her such a peculiar question.

'Daniel, wait!' She caught hold of his sleeve and stopped him as he started to walk away. He turned to face her and she saw the indecision that darkened his hazel eyes. Obviously, he was torn between a desire to get himself out of an embarrassing situation and some other pressing need. It was what that need could be which piqued Emma's curiosity.

'You must have had a good reason for asking me that, so what was it?' She held up her hand when he opened his mouth because she could tell that he was going to deny it. 'Come on, why make such a big deal of this? I mean, it's not as though you'd asked me to do something *criminal!*'

His face broke into a wry smile. 'No. Not that I could imagine you being easily persuaded into a life of crime, Emma! You're far too nice for that. Which is probably why I managed to pluck up my courage in the first place.'

'Mmm, I see,' Emma murmured, aware that her heart had zinged at the compliment. So Daniel thought she was nice, did he? It was good to know that…very good indeed!

'Look, it's crazy, trying to have a conversation in the middle of this crush,' he continued. 'There's a café not far from here. Amy and I were going to have our tea there, so how about joining us? Then I can make a clean breast of everything.'

It was impossible to resist the entreaty in his voice and Emma didn't try. She smiled back at him. 'OK. I'm starving *and* dying of curiosity so how could I possibly refuse?'

'Great!' Daniel laughed as he set Amy on her feet and took tight hold of her hand. 'Emma is going to come and have tea with us, Amy. Won't that be nice?'

The little girl nodded happily. She took hold of Emma's hand as well as they crossed the road. Emma held on tightly to the child, smiling as she felt the cold little fingers gripping hers so trustingly. She loved children and Amy was so appealing with her dark curls and Daniel's beautiful eyes. He was obviously a very caring uncle to have offered to bring the child shopping after a hard day at work. It made Emma wonder where Amy's mother was and why she had delegated the task to Daniel.

'Right, what will you have?' Daniel handed her a menu as soon as they had sat down. The café was busy but they had managed to find a table in the corner. Emma glanced at the menu and quickly made up her mind.

'Sausage and chips, please. And a pot of tea,' she added.

Daniel shook his head. 'You nurses and your tea! I wonder if anyone has ever totted up how many gallons of the stuff is drunk each day in the average hospital?'

'I've never noticed any of the doctors refusing a cup when it's offered,' she replied tartly. 'You included!'

'All right, I hold up my hands and admit it—I am a tea-aholic!' Daniel laughed softly. A smile lightened his normally serious expression. 'You'll be telling me next to stand up and declare that my name is Daniel and I'm a tea addict!'

'What's an addict, Uncle Daniel?' Amy piped up curiously.

'It's someone who likes something very much even when it isn't really good for them,' he explained simply.

'Like when I ask you if I can have some chocolate and you tell me that it isn't good for me?' Amy frowned thoughtfully. 'But you drink lots and lots of cups of tea. Aren't they good for you?'

'Probably not, poppet. I'll have to be more careful in future, won't I?'

Daniel's tone was rueful as he exchanged a speaking look with Emma. She hid her smile, thinking how good he was with the little girl. The waitress arrived to take their order then Amy asked if she could go and look at the Christmas tree that had been set up in the window of the café.

Daniel sighed as he watched his niece run over to stand in front of it. 'She's so excited about it being Christmas. It makes me more determined that it's going to be special for her this year, despite what's happened.'

Emma frowned. 'What do you mean?'

Daniel picked up his knife and toyed with it. 'Amy's mother was killed in May. She was driving home from work when a lorry went out of control and ran into her car.'

'Oh, how dreadful!' Emma's soft grey eyes darkened with pain.

'It was.' Daniel sighed as he put the knife back on the table. 'Claire was only twenty-six and I still can't believe that she's gone. She was my sister, you see, and we were very close. Our parents were quite old when they married and they had us rather late in life. When they died it brought Claire and me even closer because we were all the family we had.'

'I can imagine,' Emma said softly, although maybe that wasn't quite true. She'd never had a family of her own—no brothers, sisters or parents—so she couldn't *really* know how it felt to form such a bond. However, she didn't want to discuss her situation right then.

'So what happened to Amy afterwards? I take it that she's living with her father?'

'No.' Daniel's tone was flat yet she heard the undercurrent of anger it held. It surprised her because he always seemed so in control. However, there was no denying the depth of his feelings as he looked over to where Amy was standing, entranced, before the shimmering silver Christmas tree.

'Claire wasn't married and she never told me who Amy's father was. They split up before Amy was born and he's never seen her.' Daniel's tone was harsh. 'It appears that he was married, only he forgot to mention that fact to Claire. The truth only emerged after she'd told him that she was pregnant. He didn't want anything to do with her or the baby after that.'

'No! Oh, how awful for her,' Emma exclaimed sadly.

'Yes. I can't imagine how any man could be so callous about his own child.' Daniel made an obvious effort to collect himself. 'Anyway, the long and the short of it is that Claire had appointed me as Amy's guardian when she was born so naturally I took responsibility for her after the accident.

'I was working in London at the time but it was out of the question to uproot Amy and take her there to live. That's why I applied for the job at St Luke's when it came up and moved here to Clearsea. At least, Amy still has contact with her friends and is living in a place she knows.'

It must have meant a lot of sacrifice for him to give up his life in the city and move to the small town. Emma was filled with admiration for him and said so.

'Not many people would have done that, Daniel. You gave up your own life to come here and take care of your niece. It must have been hard.'

'Not at all.' His face softened as he looked at the child. 'So long as Amy has everything she needs then that's all I ask. My only aim is to make sure that she's properly cared for. It's what Claire would have wanted me to do and I won't let her down.'

It couldn't be easy, though, looking after a small child and keeping up with the demands of his job, Emma thought. She knew how hard all the registrars worked, and Max Dennison was a particularly hard taskmaster. Maybe it explained why Daniel had been so reluctant to socialise since he'd started work at the hospital. With Amy to look after, his free time must be extremely limited.

'I still think it's wonderful that you should put your life on hold for Amy,' Emma said sincerely.

'It isn't a problem.' Daniel shrugged dismissively. 'I was happy to do it and I get a great deal of enjoyment out of being with her as well. Amy is a great little kid, and she's been really brave since Claire died. That's why it's so important to me that she has a wonderful Christmas. It's bound to be hard for her because she misses her mother, but I'm trying to keep things as normal as they would have been if Claire had still been here.'

He sat back with a weary sigh. 'The trouble is that I'm not Claire. I just can't do the things she used to do for Amy.'

'Which is why you asked me if I could sew?' Emma looked expectantly at him and he grinned ruefully.

'Mmm, you catch on fast, Emma Graham. But, then, I've noticed that before at work. You seem to know what a patient wants almost before she knows it herself!'

Emma felt herself blush at the compliment. It meant a lot to her because Daniel was so good at his own job. 'Thank you. Anyway, exactly what is it that you need sewn?' she said hurriedly, not wanting to dwell on how it had made her feel to hear him say that.

'An angel costume.' Daniel rolled his eyes as he saw her stunned expression. 'I knew I shouldn't have asked!'

'Don't be silly! I was just a bit surprised, that's all. I was imagining something like sewing on a button or...or darning socks!' she explained faintly.

'Do people still darn socks in this high-tech world?' The

look on his face was so comical that Emma burst out laughing.

'I doubt it. And for your information, no, I'm sure I'd be a very *bad* darner! In fact, making an angel costume sounds a far better deal to me. Just tell me what you need it for.'

'The school nativity play. Amy is an angel, and although I've managed to put together some pretty nifty wings and a halo there's no way that I and a sewing machine see eye to eye.' Daniel paused as the waitress arrived with their pot of tea.

Emma picked it up. 'Shall I pour?' She filled their cups, adding a little sugar to her own cup before sliding the bowl across the table to him.

'Thanks.' He added three large spoonfuls to his tea and stirred it thoughtfully. Emma tried not to smile but she couldn't help it. 'What?' he asked with a frown.

'Three spoons of sugar?' she teased.

He grimaced as he picked up his cup. 'I know. I keep trying to cut down but…' His rueful laugh made her laugh as well.

He put the cup back on its saucer and sighed. 'Anyway, enough of my foibles. Back to this wretched costume. I had hoped to get a local dressmaker to make it but the poor woman has broken her arm. I'm absolutely desperate and I don't know where to turn.'

'When exactly is the nativity play?' Emma asked with a frown.

'The day after tomorrow,' he replied dryly.

'Thursday?' She looked at him aghast.

'I know. It doesn't give me much time. I only found out last night about Mrs Walsh's accident and I've been in a panic ever since, which is why I threw caution to the winds and accosted you!'

He laughed but Emma could tell how worried he was. No wonder. Finding someone prepared to make Amy a costume in such a short space of time would be an impossible task at this time of the year.

Emma took a deep breath but there was no way that she could refuse to help in the circumstances. 'I'm not the world's most brilliant sewer but I'll give it a go if you want me to.'

'Would you? Really?' Daniel could barely hide his delight. He reached over the table and squeezed her hand. 'I don't know how to thank you, Emma.'

'Is Emma your girlfriend, Uncle Daniel?' a small voice piped.

'No, I'm afraid not.' Daniel let go of Emma's hand and she let out the breath she hadn't known she'd been holding. Under cover of the table she ran her hand down her skirt, feeling the faint tingling sensation in her fingers. It bothered her that Daniel's touch should have left such an impression on her because she didn't understand it.

She fixed a determined smile to her face as Amy came and sat beside her. The child's face was tinged with disappointment as she looked from Emma to her uncle. 'Oh. I thought she was because you were holding hands. Jamie said that his mummy and daddy always hold hands 'cos they love one another.'

'I, um, well, that's nice, poppet.' Daniel looked a shade embarrassed. However, he soon recovered his composure. Maybe the thought of him being in love with her had thrown him for a moment, but it hadn't made any lasting impression, Emma thought, then wondered why the idea had stung a little.

She forced herself to concentrate as he quickly explained to his niece that Emma had agreed to make her costume.

'And it will be ready for the play?' Amy asked immediately. 'It's on Thursday…that's not tomorrow but the next day after tomorrow,' she explained carefully.

'I know. Which means that I shall have to set to work on it as soon as possible.'

'I don't suppose you could start tonight?' Daniel put in quickly. 'You could come home with us after we've finished here and then you could cut it out or measure it or whatever you need to do. Of course, you might already have plans for this evening,' he added as an afterthought.

'I haven't.' Emma took a deep breath because it felt as though she had just stepped onto a roller-coaster and was being hurtled along. Half an hour ago she had been on her way to do some shopping, before spending the evening watching television. Now it seemed that she was to spend the evening with Daniel and his niece!

She smiled as the waitress arrived with their meals. 'We'd better eat up. We have a lot to do this evening!'

Daniel's home was a surprise. When they pulled up in front of the modern little semi on one of the new developments on the outskirts of the town, Emma couldn't help thinking that it was the last place she would have expected him to live. However, she didn't remark on it as she got out of the car and waited while he helped Amy out of the back seat. Hunting in his pocket for his keys, he unlocked the front door.

'Come on in. And excuse the mess. Mornings are a bit hectic in this household and I haven't had time to clear up, with going into town,' he explained, leading the way along the hall.

Opening the door to the living room, he stepped aside. Emma went into the room and took a long look around, but if she'd hoped to find any clue as to what made Daniel tick through his surroundings she would have been sorely disappointed.

Daniel laughed softly as he followed her into the room. 'I think the best way to describe it is very *beige.*'

Emma chuckled at that. 'Well, it certainly seems to be the predominant colour! Do I take it that it's a favourite of yours?'

'No way!' Daniel rolled his eyes. 'I inherited it when I moved in. This was the show house so the furniture and fittings came as part of the package. If and when I ever get time I intend to paint the walls shocking pink or…or puce. Anything but this uniform beige colour!'

Emma smiled as she took another look round the small room. The walls were a pale shade of beige, the fitted carpet a darker shade. Even the suite was beige, although there were a few brightly coloured cushions scattered across it which helped to relieve the monotony.

'I imagine it's hard, finding time to decorate, with everything else you have to do,' she observed lightly.

'It is. There just aren't enough hours in the day, to be honest. Anyway, give me your coat then I'll find the material and show you what the costume is supposed to look like.'

He took her coat, shooing Amy upstairs to fetch the material. Emma sat on the sofa until they came back. She didn't have to wait very long.

'This is it.' Daniel shook out a length of white cotton fabric for her inspection then hunted a piece of paper out of the bag it had been wrapped in. 'And this is how the costume is supposed to look when it's finished.'

Emma took the paper from him and studied the design. It looked quite simple, thankfully enough, little more than a long-sleeved T-shirt from what she could tell, although it would need to be long enough to reach Amy's feet.

'That doesn't look too difficult,' she observed thoughtfully. 'It's pretty basic and shouldn't take long to make once it's cut out.'

'Won't it? Oh, that's great!' Daniel didn't try to hide his relief and Emma smiled.

'A weight off your mind, I can tell,' she teased.

'A ton weight and I don't mind admitting it.' He looked at Amy and his hazel eyes sparkled with laughter. 'Hopefully, you won't have to wear a bed sheet wrapped around you after all, sprog!'

'You wouldn't really have made me wear a sheet, would you, Uncle Daniel?' Amy asked worriedly.

He bent and hugged her. 'Of course I wouldn't! I was just teasing you. Now, will you go and fetch Mummy's sewing basket for Emma, please?'

He sighed as the little girl hurried away. 'I sometimes forget how literally children take things. I must be more careful what I say in future. I certainly don't want Amy worrying unnecessarily because of some chance remark I've made.'

'It must be hard, adapting.' Emma hurried on when he looked quizzically at her. She hoped that he wouldn't think she was being presumptuous but she didn't enjoy watching him blaming himself when there was no need. 'Bringing up a child isn't easy, especially when you have been thrust in at the deep end, so to speak.'

'No, I suppose not. I'm so aware of my responsibilities that I probably worry more than I should do about getting everything right.' He smiled. 'Thanks, Emma. I shall bear that in mind in future and not keep giving myself such a hard time. I want to be the perfect parent but I'm probably causing myself more headaches than if I took a more relaxed approach!'

Amy came back just then so the subject was dropped. However, as she got out the tape measure, Emma couldn't help hoping that Daniel would do as he'd said he would. It was a shame if he was putting so much pressure on himself when he was doing such a wonderful job.

She sighed as she jotted down Amy's measurements on a scrap of paper. She doubted if Daniel would appreciate her concern! He had always struck her as a man who was very much in control of his own life.

Once she had the measurements she needed, Emma rolled up the tape measure and put it back in the sewing basket. 'I think I've got everything I need now. Obviously, I'll have to make the dress then check that it fits properly, but we don't have a lot of time to spare before the play.'

'Maybe you could come here for tea tomorrow?' Daniel suggested promptly. He laughed when Amy clapped her hands. 'Obviously, Amy thinks it's a good idea as well.'

'Will you, Emma? Will you come again tomorrow?' Amy demanded eagerly.

'Well, yes, of course. If that's what you want.' Emma tried to temper the small glow of happiness with a large dose of common sense. Naturally, Daniel was eager to invite her to his home again when she had to make sure Amy's costume fitted her. However, when he smiled at her she couldn't help wondering if it was *only* because of her dressmaking skills that he'd issued the invitation…

'It is. If the costume doesn't fit then you'll be right here on the spot to make any alterations.' His tone was pleasant enough but it pricked her bubble like a pin stuck into a balloon.

Emma busied herself with fastening the sewing basket so that he wouldn't see how disappointed she felt. How silly of her to feel like that! Daniel had invited her here purely for his niece's sake. There had been nothing *personal* about the invitation. It had been purely practical.

'So, you're pretty confident that you can make the costume in time?' he asked as she stood up.

'I can't see it will be that difficult,' she told him quietly, hoping her voice wouldn't betray her disappointment. 'I'll cut it out when I get home and it shouldn't take more than a couple of hours to sew it all together.'

'Which means that most of your evening will be taken up doing it. Obviously, I shall pay you for your time and trouble, Emma,' he offered at once.

She shook her head, feeling a little bit hurt that he should imagine she wanted payment. 'Don't be silly. I'm happy to do it.'

'Are you sure?' Daniel persisted. 'I'm sure you can think of a lot better things to do with your free time rather than slaving over a sewing machine!'

'It isn't a problem. Really.' Emma quickly folded up the fabric and popped it back in its bag. 'Right, I think that's everything I need now.'

'I'll drive you home.' Daniel shook his head when she opened her mouth to tell him there was no need. 'No, I insist. It's the least I can do after you've been so kind.'

He went to fetch his coat so Emma didn't protest any further. Amy skipped down the path ahead of them and got into the car. Daniel made sure her seat belt was securely fastened then helped Emma into the passenger seat.

It didn't take them long to drive back into town. Emma's flat was on the top floor of one of the old Victorian houses facing the sea front. Daniel peered up at the house then looked across the road. The tide was coming in and they could hear it lapping at the shore now that the car had stopped.

'You must have a great view from here. I love these old houses. They are so full of character, aren't they?'

'Too full of it sometimes,' Emma replied ruefully. 'You try dealing with the quirks of ancient plumbing when you're in a rush to get ready for work! Take it from me, there's nothing to beat a nice modern bathroom with hot and cold water running *every* time you turn on a tap!'

'I shall bear that in mind! Maybe there's something to be said for modern houses after all.'

'Why did you choose to live where you do if you're not a fan of new houses?' she asked curiously.

'Because it's close to Amy's school and where all her friends live,' he replied simply. 'It made more sense to buy a property there.'

Even though it wouldn't have been his ideal choice if the circumstances had been different, Emma thought. It struck her once again just how much he'd been prepared to sacrifice for the sake of his niece. However, she didn't say anything as she opened the car door because she knew that he would be embarrassed to hear her praise him again.

'I'd better let you get home,' she said instead, stepping out of the car. She paused to smile at the child before closing the door. 'Bye, Amy. I'll see you tomorrow.'

'Thanks again for everything, Emma. I really do appreciate it, you know.' Daniel leaned over to speak to her. His face was lit by the glow from a nearby streetlight and Emma felt her heart roll over as she thought how handsome he looked as he smiled up at her.

She smiled back, praying that he wouldn't notice anything amiss. 'You're very welcome. I…I'll see you tomorrow, then.'

He raised his hand in acknowledgement then started the engine as she slammed the car door. Emma stood on the pavement and watched as he drove away. There was a funny bubbly feeling in the pit of her stomach, a sort of nervous excitement. She couldn't recall ever feeling anything like it before, apart from when she'd sat her final exams…

She gave a snort of disgust as she let herself into the house. Equating Daniel Hutton's effect on her with an attack of exam nerves just showed what a sorry state her life was in! It was her own fault, of course. She'd had her fair share of invitations from various male members of staff at St Luke's but, increasingly, she'd found herself turning them down. What was she holding out for? A knight in shining armour to come along on his white charger and carry her off to his castle? Huh!

Emma hurried up the stairs to her flat, annoyed with herself for the way she'd been behaving recently. Dropping her bag onto a chair, she went to haul out the sewing machine from the bottom of her wardrobe and set it up in the living room. The sooner she got this done, the better. Then she would start making a few changes to her life. She would do what most of her friends had done and settle for some pleasant man. No more waiting around for a knight to show up. They tended to be very thin on the ground!

Unbidden, a face sprang to mind and she sighed. Daniel Hutton would make a perfect knight in shining armour but he was way out of her league!

CHAPTER THREE

'WHAT were you up to last night? You must have been doing something to put those bags under your eyes, Emma Graham. Come on, tell!'

Emma sighed as she heard the speculation in Linda's voice. It was just gone seven and she was already late arriving for work. Taking a clean white uniform top out of her locker, she popped it over her head and smoothed it down over her trim hips. 'I stayed up late, sewing, if you must know.'

'Sewing?' Linda parroted. She folded her arms and stared at Emma. 'You can do better than that! Nobody looks like that after a night spent *sewing!*'

'They do if they've stayed up till one o'clock in the morning, trying to get it finished,' Emma informed her tartly. She quickly laced up her regulation shoes then headed for the door. 'Come on. Sister will have a fit if we don't get a move on.'

Linda shook her head. 'Oh, no, you don't! I intend to get to the bottom of this before we set one foot out of this staffroom. What were you sewing? And why did you need to stay up so late to get it finished?'

Emma sighed as she realised that she'd painted herself into a corner. Did she really want to tell Linda that she'd stayed up late, making a costume for Daniel's niece? It would be bound to lead to more questions and the thought of betraying his confidence by telling Linda about his sister and everything was out of the question. If Daniel had wanted people to know about his private affairs, he would have told them.

'I just wanted to get it done, that's all,' she hedged.

31

'But it must have been something special.' Linda was like a dog with the proverbial bone as she scented a juicy story. 'What was it? A new dress for the dance, perhaps? I didn't think you were coming. Have you decided to go with Mike Humphreys after all?'

'I…um, yes.' Emma groaned as she was pushed into telling the fib. Mike Humphreys was a houseman on Max Dennison's team and he'd asked her to go to the Christmas dance with him a few days previously. Emma had been caught off guard and had ended up promising to think about it because she hadn't been able to come up with an excuse. Now she might have no choice but to accept Mike's invitation just to give credence to her lie!

'Good for you! It's about time you had some fun.' Linda was full of enthusiasm as they hurriedly made their way into the ward. Luckily, Sister Carter was busy in her office, taking an incoming call, so she didn't see them arriving. She was a tartar about time-keeping and woe betide any members of staff who didn't arrive at least five minutes before their shift was officially due to commence.

Emma began her round of the ward, checking the obs that the night staff had done. The patients had been given their breakfasts and Linda's first task of the day was to clear away the dirty dishes. She managed to do so and keep up with Emma as she made her way from bed to bed.

'So, what made you decide to go to the dance in the end?' her friend persisted, piling cups and bowls haphazardly onto the trolley.

'Oh, I just thought I may as well.' Emma shrugged, hoping that Linda would take the hint and not keep asking questions. It was a vain hope, of course, because her friend had no intention of letting the subject drop.

'Actually, Mike's quite fanciable if you like that little-boy-lost type. Of course, he isn't Daniel Hutton but, then, who is?' Linda whisked Jean Horrocks's cup and saucer off her locker and dumped them on the pile of crockery.

'Now, there's a man I'd stay up sewing for…or anything else for that matter!'

'You and me both, love,' Jean Horrocks put in. 'He's got those lovely come-to-bed eyes, hasn't he? Makes me go all shivery, just thinking about him.'

Emma had to bite her lip to hold back a snappy reproof. For some reason she resented hearing them talk about Daniel that way. She picked up Jean's chart then paused as it hit her that she might be jealous. Surely not. What right did she have to feel jealous about Daniel?

'Nothing wrong, is there, Staff? I did feel a bit woozy through the night and wondered if it was my blood pressure being too high. Or maybe too low. I read something in a magazine about that—it said it was really dangerous!'

Emma gathered her scattered wits as she heard the panic in Jean's voice. 'There is nothing wrong, Mrs Horrocks. Your blood pressure and everything else is fine. I…I was just checking that your notes were up to date, that's all.'

'And what could have gone wrong when you had dishy Daniel to do your op?' put in the irrepressible Linda.

'Nothing, of course. Silly of me to go worrying, wasn't it?' Jean Horrocks smiled at the mention of Daniel's name. 'I told him straight, I did, that I was more than happy to leave myself in his capable hands. Is he married, do you know, love?'

'No idea. Dr Hutton is the original mystery man and plays his cards very close to his chest,' Linda replied cheerfully. 'So if you find out anything about him, Mrs Horrocks, do let us know. We shall all be eternally grateful to you!'

Emma moved away. She was glad when Linda got delayed as Jean asked her another question. Maybe she was being overly sensitive but all this talk about Daniel's private life was starting to grate.

People should mind their own business, she thought crossly, then realised that it was natural curiosity which had prompted the speculation. She should see it as that and not get too defensive. After all, Daniel hadn't asked her to keep their meeting a secret so there was no real reason why she shouldn't have mentioned it. However, it felt wrong to start spreading gossip about him.

The morning flew past. There was a bit of panic just before break-time when an emergency case was sent up from A and E. Paula Walters, a woman in her mid-thirties, had been rushed in by ambulance when she'd started haemorrhaging. She'd been at work when it had happened and was doubly distressed by the thought of her colleagues having witnessed what had gone on.

She'd lost a fair amount of blood and the staff in A and E had set up a drip. However, they'd been too busy to deal with the problem any further, which was why Paula had been sent straight to the ward.

Emma got her settled then checked that the intravenous line was working properly. Paula hadn't said much since she'd been brought to the ward. She seemed a little dazed by what had happened, which was no wonder.

Emma smiled reassuringly at her. 'You'll feel a lot better once your fluid level is back to what it should be. And the doctor will be here soon to examine you.'

'Can you get a message to my fiancé? I was supposed to meet him for lunch and he'll be worried.' Paula's eyes filled. 'We were going to the registrar's office to book our wedding, you see.'

'Of course. Can you give me a number where I can reach him?' Emma asked at once.

'In my diary…under Edmonds. Stephen Edmonds.' Paula pointed to her bag which was lying on top of her bedside locker. Emma opened it and found the diary. She made a note of the telephone number then put the diary back.

'I'll put your bag in this locker,' she told Paula. 'It's always safer not to leave valuables lying around.'

'Thanks. My engagement ring is in it so I don't want to

take any chances.' Paula managed a shaky smile. 'Stephen and I were taking it in to the jeweller's to have it made smaller as it's a bit loose.'

'Sister could put it in the safe in her office, if you'd prefer,' Emma offered immediately, but Paula shook her head.

'Thanks, but I'd like to keep it with me.' Tears welled into her eyes all of a sudden. 'I feel so awful about what happened. I was in the middle of this big meeting and I was the only woman there. How on earth am I going to face everyone again?'

'I shouldn't worry about that, Paula,' Emma said quickly. 'I know it must have been embarrassing for you, but it's just one of those things. Your main concern at the moment is to get yourself well again. Have you had any problems like this in the past?'

'Have I!' Paula sighed. 'I've come to dread the time when my period is due. It's got to the point where it lasts for a couple of weeks and it's so heavy that I live in fear of my clothes getting stained.'

Emma frowned. 'What has your GP said?'

Paula looked embarrassed. 'I haven't been to see him. I've been so busy with work that I don't seem to have the time to spare. I've just kept plodding on, hoping that a miracle would happen.'

'Unfortunately, miracles are rather rare,' Emma observed dryly, earning herself a rueful smile from the other woman.

'I know. I've been very silly but I've learned my lesson. I won't be such a fool about my health in the future, believe me!'

'Good. Now just try to relax. The doctor will be here very shortly to examine you.'

Emma drew the curtains around the bed. She sighed as she went to check what Sister Carter wanted her to do next. How many times had she heard a similar story since she'd started working on the obs and gynae unit? Far too many women dismissed the problems they were having because they were so busy trying to do a hundred jobs at once. When you were mother, lover, home-maker and wage-earner all rolled into one, it was hard to find time for yourself.

Max Dennison arrived for his ward round a short time later so he examined Paula. Sister Carter accompanied him but she'd asked Emma to make sure that the patient was ready, which was how Emma happened to be by the bed when the team arrived. She acknowledged Mr Dennison's curt nod then felt her stomach give a little jolt as she saw that Daniel was with him.

'Good morning, Staff,' he said formally, although there was a bit more warmth in his smile than she'd ever seen before.

'Dr Hutton,' she replied equally formally. She moved away from the bed as Mr Dennison went to take his place, holding the curtain open so that the others could follow him. Daniel hung back, letting Sister Carter and Mike Humphreys go ahead of him. There was a hint of concern on his face as he studied the dark circles under Emma's eyes.

'I hope you didn't stay up too late last night, sewing Amy's costume,' he said quietly, so that the others couldn't hear.

Emma shrugged. 'Not that late.'

He sighed. 'I feel awful now. It wasn't fair to put you on the spot like that.'

'Rubbish! If I hadn't wanted to help, I wouldn't have offered.' She caught Sister's eye and quickly moved out of the way, but she couldn't help smiling when she thought about how quick Daniel had been to spot the signs of tiredness on her face. Obviously, he noticed things like that about her...

Of course he did! He was a doctor, wasn't he? He was trained to spot symptoms and draw conclusions. The fact that he had homed in on her tiredness didn't mean that he took a *personal* interest in how she looked!

It was a sobering thought and it helped to show her how foolishly she was behaving. Daniel had asked for her help simply because there had been no one else to ask. She had to put what had happened into that context and not start spinning silly little fantasies around it.

She had managed to talk some sense into herself by the time she went for lunch. Linda went with her and she groaned as she read the day's menu chalked up on the board by the door.

'Fish pie! Oh, shoot the chef, someone…please!'

Emma laughed. 'Fish is good for you,' she teased. 'It's slimming, full of vitamins and wonderful brain food.'

'Maybe it is, but give me a nice big juicy burger and chips any day of the week!' Linda picked up a package of sandwiches and plonked it despondently on her tray. She suddenly brightened. 'Ah, there's Mike over there. Let's sit with him. Seeing as you're coming to the dance now, we could make up a foursome—you, me, Mike and Gary.'

'Oh, but…' Emma didn't get any further as Linda hurried away. She paid for her meal then slowly made her way across the canteen. It didn't help when she saw that Daniel was also sitting at the table. The thought of discussing her forthcoming date with Mike made her feel uncomfortable, although there was no reason why it should have done. Daniel Hutton had no claims on her, apart from needing her skills a seamstress!

'Hi, Em!' Mike grinned as she put her tray on the table. He hauled out a chair so that she had little choice but to sit next to him. However, she was deeply conscious of Daniel, watching her from across the table as she sat down.

She looked up but he avoided her eyes as he turned to Linda. 'So the four of you are going to make a night of it, then?'

'Yes. It should be good fun. The hospital dos usually

are.' Linda pretended to have been struck by a sudden wonderful thought. 'Why don't you come, Daniel? You could come with us then you wouldn't have to be on your own—not that you'd be short of a partner for long, I imagine!'

Linda treated him to a flirtatious smile and Emma snorted in disgust. She suddenly realised that everyone had turned to look at her and she coughed.

'A bit of a tickle in my throat,' she mumbled, blushing.

'Here, have a drink of this.' Mike passed her his glass of mineral water and she obediently took a sip.

'Thanks,' she muttered, passing the glass back to him.

'You're welcome.' He lowered his voice so that the other two couldn't hear him. 'I was really chuffed when Linda told me that you'd decided to come to the dance with me, Em.'

'I…um, yes. It was good of you to invite me,' she said, trying to inject a little enthusiasm into her voice. Fortunately, Mike didn't seem to notice anything amiss but, oddly, she could tell that Daniel was watching her closely.

Did he suspect that she wasn't as keen on the idea as Mike was? she wondered, then gave herself a mental shake. Of course not!

Mike's face split into a wide smile. 'I've been going to ask you out for ages, to be honest. Some of the guys warned me that you don't go out on dates so I've been a bit cagey. However, I wish I hadn't wasted so much time now.'

There was a note of triumph in his voice and Emma sighed. Did Mike see her acceptance as a sign that he'd succeeded where all the others had failed? Probably! Although he was pleasant enough, his attitude was still rather immature so she could well imagine that he enjoyed the thought of scoring points off his friends.

'I'd better be off.' Daniel turned to the younger man. 'Don't forget that Max wants you to check on Paula Walters again this afternoon. He's hoping to schedule her for surgery once he's had the results of the ultrasound scan.'

Mike groaned. 'Oh, save me from weeping women! I can't wait to finish my stint on Obs and Gynae. Why do they make such a fuss when most of these ops are purely routine?'

'Because they aren't routine to them.' Daniel's tone was icy. 'I suggest you bear that in mind, otherwise you could find yourself being moved sooner than you expected.'

There was silence after Daniel left. Mike shrugged but there was little doubt that he was embarrassed to have been told off like that. 'That's put me in my place, hasn't it? It must be wonderful to know that you're perfect, like our Dr Hutton obviously thinks he is!'

'I don't believe that Daniel thinks any such thing,' Emma said at once, immediately springing to Daniel's defence. 'He was just pointing out that you need to treat people sensitively.'

'And, obviously, you agree with him, Emma.' Mike looked annoyed. 'Maybe it isn't a good idea, you coming with me to the dance, if that's how you feel.'

He pushed back his chair and left. Linda sighed as she watched him storming out of the canteen. 'Not very tactful, Emma. You could have at least *pretended* to be on Mike's side, seeing as he'd asked you out.'

Emma shrugged as she unwrapped her sandwich. 'I was just being truthful. If Mike doesn't like it then it's his hard luck.'

'You were rather quick to take sides, though. Come on, confess; you have a bit of a thing about our Daniel, haven't you?'

'Of course not!' she denied, too quickly. She saw Linda's brows rise and moderated her tone. The last thing she wanted was her friend throwing out hints every time Daniel set foot in the ward! 'I just happen to agree with him in this instance, that's all.'

Mercifully, that seemed to bring the subject to a close. They finished their lunch then went back to the ward. Alison Banks was being sent home that afternoon and Emma helped her pack her bag. The girl was looking a lot happier than she had been, mainly, Emma suspected, because her husband had been granted compassionate leave and would be home for Christmas. Being on your own at Christmas could be particularly hard, as she knew only too well.

Mike barely looked at her when he came to the ward to check on Paula Walters. Emma ignored his ill humour as she accompanied him to the patient's bed. If Mike chose to behave like that, it was up to him. Paula's ·fiancé, Stephen, had arrived soon after lunch and he waited outside in the corridor while Paula was examined.

Emma tidied the bed after Mike had finished then went to fetch Stephen back in. She found him looking very distressed.

'Is anything wrong, Mr Edmonds?' she asked solicitously.

'I...I hadn't realised what it meant when Paula told me that she might need an operation.'

The poor man looked so dazed that Emma knew she couldn't let him return to the ward in such a state. She quickly led him into the office and closed the door. Sister Carter had been called away to deal with a query about supplies so there was nobody in there.

'Sit down, Mr Edmonds, and tell me what this is all about.' Emma waited until he had sat down. 'Obviously, it has something to do with your fiancée's operation.'

'Yes. That young doctor...Humphreys, was it?' He carried on when Emma nodded. 'Well, he just told me that Paula is going to need a hysterectomy. I hadn't realised that was what was going to happen, you see. I mean, we're planning on getting married and we both want a family but...but that won't be possible now.'

Emma could tell how distraught he was and no wonder. She felt very angry with Mike for telling the poor man something like that then just walking off. It was unforgivable, especially as she wasn't sure that it was even true.

According to Paula's notes, there was a strong suspicion that she was suffering from fibroids, benign tumours which grew within the uterus. Her symptoms—the excessive and prolonged menstrual bleeding and tenderness in the abdomen—pointed to that, although at this stage it wasn't possible to rule out other causes, which was why Max Dennison had ordered the ultrasound scan.

However, from what Emma had read, there had been no decision made about Paula undergoing a hysterectomy. Although in very severe cases it was often considered the best method of treatment, there were other options, like a myomectomy. Removing each fibroid separately from the uterus meant that a woman's fertility would be unaffected.

She decided that she needed to speak to either Max Dennison or Daniel so that they could explain the situation to Paula's fiancé. She certainly didn't want him upsetting Paula when there might be no need.

'I'll get one of the senior doctors to have a word with you, Mr Edmonds. Just bear with me while I have them paged.'

She put through a call to the switchboard. Sister Carter popped her head round the door then nodded when Emma mouthed that she wouldn't be long. Sister believed firmly in delegating responsibility to her staff so Emma wasn't worried about overstepping her authority. She was relieved when Daniel returned her call almost immediately.

'I wonder if you could come and have a word with Paula Walter's fiancé, Dr Hutton?' she asked calmly, although she couldn't ignore the jolt her heart had given when she'd heard his voice.

'Of course. Do I take it there is a problem, Emma?'

He'd never called her by her first name at work before

and she felt herself blush. It was an effort to keep her tone level, although she heard the slightly breathless note it held even if Daniel didn't.

'I think so.'

'I'll be up straight away.' He didn't question her further but hung up. Emma went to meet him at the lift, smiling when he appeared less than two minutes later.

'You were quick,' she teased.

'Your wish is my command, ma'am!' he replied with a light laugh. He glanced towards the office and sobered. 'So, what is this all about, Emma? I know you wouldn't have called me if you weren't worried.'

She quickly explained what had gone on and how upset Stephen Edmonds was. Daniel's face was grim by the time she finished.

'What a damned stupid thing to do!' He made an obvious effort to collect himself. 'I'm sorry. I know Humphreys is your boyfriend but he had no right to give out information like that. Quite apart from the fact that it's unethical to discuss a patient's condition with a third party, what he said isn't true. Max won't decide on the best course of treatment until he's seen the results of the ultrasound.'

'That's what I thought.' Emma grimaced. 'I hope Mike won't get into trouble…'

'Don't worry. I'll make sure he doesn't find out about your involvement,' Daniel said, curtly interrupting her. 'I don't want to make things awkward for you, Emma.'

That wasn't what she'd meant but there wasn't time to correct him as Daniel excused himself and went straight to the office. Emma went back to the ward and quickly explained to Sister Carter what had gone on. The older woman immediately agreed that she'd done the right thing. When Stephen came back into the ward a short time later, looking far less stressed, Emma breathed a sigh of relief. At least Daniel had been able to set the poor man's mind at rest.

The afternoon passed without any more hiccups. Jean Horrocks was discharged and left looking like a different woman to the nervous creature who had been admitted two days earlier. However, it didn't stop her making the most of the occasion. As she left the ward, Emma could hear Jean telling her husband that she wouldn't be able to do *anything* when she got home, not after her operation, so he'd have to do all the cooking and cleaning while she rested.

Emma exchanged a wry smile with Shirley Rogers as she went to strip Jean's bed. And why not? There had to be a few perks for being a woman!

The end of the shift arrived at last and they handed over to the night staff. Emma hurried to change out of her uniform. She wasn't sure which bus she would need to catch to get to Daniel's house so she would have to go all the way into town and ask at the depot.

'You're in a rush. Got a date, then?' Linda rolled up her uniform top and thrust it unceremoniously into a carrier bag.

'No, I've just got a lot to do, that's all,' Emma explained briefly.

'Not the dress again? Does that mean you and Mike have patched things up after that little episode at lunchtime?'

'I haven't spoken to him.' Emma closed her locker then picked up her bag. She had brought Amy's costume with her to save time. She mentally crossed her fingers that it would fit the child. She didn't have enough time to make another one and she couldn't bear to imagine the little girl's disappointment.

Linda accompanied her as they left the hospital via the staff entrance. It was obvious that she was still dying to know what Emma had planned for that night. 'Do you want a lift?' she offered guilelessly. 'If you're not going straight home, maybe I could drop you off somewhere.'

'No, it's fine, thanks. I'm going into town, as it happens,

and you don't want to get caught up in the rush, do you?'
Emma hid her smile as Linda hesitated. However, common
sense finally prevailed and her friend departed.

Emma set off down the path, hoping that she hadn't
missed the bus that would take her into the town centre. St
Luke's had been built on the outskirts of the town to allow
for future expansion but it did mean that anyone working
at the hospital had to travel there by bus or car. She'd
almost reached the gates when she heard a car horn tooting
behind her.

She looked round, expecting to see Linda, and was so
surprised when she discovered that it had been Daniel trying to attract her attention that she just stared at him.

He wound down the window and stuck his head out.
'Come on, hop in. We're causing a traffic jam.'

Emma glanced up the path and flushed as she saw the
cars which had needed to stop because Daniel had done so.
She was very conscious of the interested glances being cast
her way as she hurriedly got into his car. There was little
doubt in her mind that the news would spread like wildfire
through the hospital, and how would Daniel feel about that?

'What's wrong? You look as though you've lost the proverbial pound.' He paused and there was an oddly strained
note in his voice when he continued. 'Humphreys hasn't
been giving you a hard time about helping me with Amy's
costume, has he? I was careful to keep your name out of
the conversation when I spoke to him about Paula Walters
but he wasn't pleased about being reprimanded by me twice
in one day.'

'It's got nothing to do with Mike,' Emma declared. However, it was obvious that Daniel didn't believe her.

'Hasn't it? Look, Emma, the last thing I want is to cause
problems between you and your boyfriend…'

'He isn't my boyfriend!' Emma saw Daniel look at her
and grimaced as she realised how loudly she'd said that.

However, it was way past time that she set the record straight.

'Mike invited me to the Christmas dance, that's all,' she explained more quietly.

Daniel shrugged but his face was set as he slowed for the traffic lights as they changed to red. 'If you agreed to go to the dance with him then obviously you must like him.'

'Yes, I do. Well, I did before today. But it was sort of…of casual, if you know what I mean. Mike is just some-one I work with and he's always seemed pleasant enough…' She tailed off, wishing she had left well alone. Daniel probably now thought she was the sort of woman who accepted a date from just anyone!

'But he doesn't make your heart beat faster or rockets go off?'

She had to laugh at the droll note in his voice. 'Hardly! And as for accepting the invitation, well that was more by accident than design, I'm afraid.'

'Really? You can't leave it at that, Emma. I'm dying of curiosity now.' His smile was full of amusement and she felt her breath catch. Daniel was disturbingly handsome even when he wore his usual solemn expression, but when he smiled… Well!

She looked away, afraid that her own expression might be too revealing. 'It was a mix-up, that's all. Linda wanted to know why I looked so tired this morning and I told her that I'd stayed up late, sewing. Somehow she got it into her head that I'd been making a new dress for the dance.'

'And she knew that Mike had asked you to go with him and so it snowballed from there?' Daniel's tone was wry. 'It seems to me that I've caused you an awful lot of prob-lems, Emma. I'm sorry.'

'It doesn't matter. I could have told her the truth, of course, but I wasn't sure if you wanted people to know about your private affairs.' She shrugged when he glanced at her. 'You've kept yourself very much to yourself since you started at St Luke's.'

'I have. And that has been more by accident than design as well. I simply don't have time for a private life any more, with Amy to look after. It's easier not to get involved.'

Did that mean that he wasn't planning on getting involved in a relationship? The thought was unsettling, although it really wasn't any of her business. What Daniel did with his life was his affair. Yet it was one thing to know that and another to accept it.

'Anyway, I don't want you being put under pressure like that again, Emma. The fact that I am looking after Amy isn't a secret. People are bound to find out.'

They had reached the estate where he lived by then. He drew up in front of a semi very similar to his own and turned to her as he switched off the engine. 'Amy stays with a childminder after school. It's the same person Claire always used so she's quite happy with the arrangement. I'll fetch her then we can go home.'

'Fine.' Emma agreed. She watched as Daniel strode up the path and knocked on the door. It was a relief to know that she didn't have to keep everything a secret, although that didn't mean she intended to start spreading gossip, of course.

She sighed as she remembered all the curious eyes watching her as she'd got into his car that night. The gossip mill would already have started working if she knew anything about the hospital! Yet what was there to gossip about exactly? All she'd done had been to agree to make a costume for Daniel's niece. Once she'd checked that it fitted Amy, that would be that. Daniel wouldn't need her help any longer, would he?

She felt a sudden painful tug at her heart as she watched him coming down the path with Amy. She couldn't help wishing that she could be part of his life for a lot longer than just one day.

CHAPTER FOUR

'Oh, it's beautiful! Look, Uncle Daniel…look at me!'

Emma smiled as Amy went rushing out of the room to find her uncle. The angel costume had proved to be a perfect fit and Emma was delighted that her hard work hadn't been in vain. She stood up as Daniel came into the room, smiling as she saw the astonishment on his face.

'How on earth did you manage to make it look so good in such a short time?' Daniel fingered the silver trim Emma had stitched so carefully around the neck and edges of the sleeves. 'It must have taken you hours of sewing.'

Emma shrugged modestly. 'It wasn't all that difficult. Once I'd got it cut out, it was just a question of stitching it all together. I still have to do the hem because I didn't want to take a chance on getting the length wrong.'

'Can I put my wings and hello on, Uncle Daniel… please?' Amy demanded.

'It's a halo, sprog,' he gently corrected her. 'You can try them on after we've had tea. It's almost ready now so why don't you take off your costume and set the table?'

Amy sighed. 'All right. But I can put it on again later, can't I? Promise?'

'Cross my heart!' Daniel made a cross over his heart and Amy laughed. She let Emma help her out of the costume then ran out of the room and they could hear the sound of cutlery clattering as she set about laying the table.

Daniel picked up the gown and examined the neatly sewn seams. 'I'm amazed. A dressmaker couldn't have made a better job than you have, Emma. Where did you learn to sew like this?'

'I taught myself.' She smiled reminiscently as she stowed

the offcuts of cloth back in the bag. 'I was so hard up when I left the home that I couldn't afford to buy any clothes so I made them instead. It was so much cheaper.'

'The home? What do you mean by that?' Daniel frowned as he carefully laid the costume over the back of a chair.

'I was brought up in care and lived in a children's home until I was sixteen,' Emma explained quietly, wondering how he would react to the information. People were usually curious when they found out about her background, wanting to know all the details.

'Really?' He captured her hands, holding them lightly as he studied her. 'That must have been hard for you. I imagine the worst thing of all is the lack of permanency in your life when you're brought up in care.'

Emma blinked because she'd never expected him to say that. The people who'd run the home had been kind enough and all the children living there had been well cared for. However, the staff had changed so frequently that there had been no question of forming a bond with any of them. It surprised her that Daniel had understood that so quickly.

'It was. I used to envy my school friends because they had mums and dads who were always there for them. Oh, they got told off sometimes but they knew that no matter what they did their parents would still love them.' She sighed softly. 'I envied them that, even though I'd never known what it was like to be part of a real family.'

Daniel was still holding her hands and she felt his fingers tighten. She had a feeling that what she'd said had touched him. 'So you never knew your parents, Emma?'

'No. I was a foundling, would you believe? I was left on the steps of a police station when I was a few hours old!' She laughed because she'd learned a long time ago that it was better to make a joke of the circumstances surrounding her birth. People were either embarrassed or overly curious when they found out, and she preferred not to have to deal with either if she could avoid it. However, surprisingly, Daniel seemed more upset than anything else.

'How awful! I can't imagine what would drive a woman to abandon her baby like that!'

His hazel eyes shimmered with concern and Emma felt her heart warm. She'd long since accepted what had happened, though it still hurt at times. However, it was good to know that Daniel genuinely cared.

'Maybe my mother had no choice,' she said softly. 'I try not to think about why she did it. I just focus on the thought that she must have cared otherwise she wouldn't have taken such trouble to leave me somewhere I'd be found.'

'You're right, of course.' Daniel smiled at her and his eyes were tender. 'Trust you to find something good about the situation, though, Emma. It's so typical of you.'

He let her go, obviously not expecting her to say anything. Emma was glad because she wasn't sure what she might have come up with. Had that been meant as a compliment?

A smile played around her mouth at the thought, although she knew that it was foolish to go reading too much into what had been probably just a passing comment. However, there was a definite spring in her step as she followed Daniel to the kitchen.

'Can I help?' Emma offered, sniffing appreciatively as she caught the waft of some deliciously spicy odour.

'Nope. You sit yourself down. You've done more than enough in the past twenty-four hours. It's time that Amy and I showed our appreciation!'

Daniel's tone was teasing as he drew out a chair with a flourish for her to sit on. Emma laughed as he draped a piece of kitchen towel across her knee in his best imitation of a waiter in a high-class restaurant.

'Well, if the food is as good as the service has been so far then I won't have any complaints,' she teased.

He waggled his eyebrows at her. 'You won't taste food

better than this anywhere in the whole of Clearsea. The chef is a genius. What he doesn't know about microwaving isn't worth mentioning!'

Emma shook her head. 'And here was I thinking that you'd been slaving over a hot stove, too.'

'Listen, it isn't easy, operating a microwave.' Daniel treated her to a stern look. 'First you have to read the instructions very carefully. Then you have to set the timer. Then you have to arrange the food on the plates…'

Emma held up her hands. 'I take it back! I can see just how difficult it is now.'

'We don't usually have plates,' Amy whispered conspiratorially. 'We usually eat our tea out of the plastic dishes 'cos Uncle Daniel says that it saves having to wash—'

'Shoo! Away with you, wretched child. Don't give away all our secrets!' Daniel scooped Amy up and threw her over his shoulder, making the little girl laugh uproariously. Emma joined in because there was no way she could resist. It was obvious that Daniel had a very close and loving relationship with his niece and that Amy adored him. She couldn't help thinking how lucky the little girl had been when her mother had died to have had Daniel to take care of her.

They lingered over the surprisingly tasty spaghetti Bolognese and salad that Daniel served. Amy had ice cream afterwards but Emma was too full to eat anything else so she just had a cup of coffee.

'That was excellent. My compliments to the chef…and his microwave.' She smiled as Daniel brought his coffee to the table and sat down. Amy had finished her ice cream and had gone into the sitting room to watch a cartoon on the video player.

'Thank you, although I think the microwave deserves more of the credit than the chef does.' Daniel sighed all of a sudden. 'Actually, joking apart, I do feel guilty that I don't cook more than a couple of times a week. Claire was always so careful about what Amy ate.'

'There was absolutely nothing wrong with the meal you served tonight,' Emma assured him quickly. 'You can't do everything, Daniel. You're doing your best and, from what I've seen so far, that's more than enough.'

'Think so?' He smiled when she nodded. 'Thanks. It's nice to hear you say that. It makes me realise how hard it must have been for Claire these past six years, bringing Amy up on her own.'

'She didn't meet anyone else after Amy's father left her?' Emma asked softly.

He shook his head. 'No. I think Claire was so hurt by what had happened that she didn't want to risk getting involved again. It was a shame because she was a lovely person.'

'Understandable, though,' Emma remarked.

'Mmm.' He stirred his coffee thoughtfully. 'A bad experience can put you off, can't it?'

Emma wasn't sure if that had been a general observation or not. Had Daniel had a bad experience with a woman in the past, perhaps? It made her wonder if his disinclination to socialise might not be solely because of his time being limited through taking care of Amy.

It was an intriguing thought but there was no way that she could question him about it. They drank their coffee, and while Daniel was clearing up she went into the living room and hemmed the angel costume. Naturally, Amy was eager to try it on again and this time she was allowed to put on the silver cardboard wings and halo as well.

Daniel stepped back and studied his niece. 'Perfect. You're going to be the prettiest angel in the play.'

Amy did a twirl so that the folds of the gown floated out around her and her wings fluttered. 'It's lovely. Thank you, Uncle Daniel.' She rushed over and kissed him then turned to Emma. 'Thank you, Emma.'

Emma gave the child a hug, taking care not to bend the wings. 'You're welcome, darling. I hope you have a wonderful time in your play tomorrow.'

'Will you come and watch me?' Amy's face had lit up as the idea had suddenly occurred to her. 'Please, Emma, will you?'

'Well, I don't know…' Emma began, not sure how to extricate herself without causing the child any distress. However, Daniel was quick to step in.

'What a lovely idea! Clever you for thinking of it, Amy.' He turned to Emma. 'Is there any chance at all that you could get the afternoon off?'

'I do have a half-day owing…' she began then shook her head. She really didn't want Daniel to feel that he *had* to ask her. 'But I'm sure you don't really want me to come.'

'Of course we do. Don't we, Amy?' Daniel laughed as Amy enthusiastically agreed. 'That's two against one, Emma. You're outvoted!'

She shrugged, although she couldn't stop her heart from swelling with happiness at the thought of spending more time with him and his adorable niece. 'All right, then. I'll ask Sister Carter in the morning if she can spare me.'

Daniel sent Amy upstairs to hang up her costume. He insisted on driving Emma home afterwards. She was a bit disappointed that he didn't ask her to stay longer until it struck her that he needed to put Amy to bed.

Emma spent the rest of the evening watching television but her mind was never far away from what was going to happen the following day. An afternoon with Daniel was something to look forward to and it delayed the moment when he wouldn't need her help any more. Funnily enough, she knew that she would really miss not being with him and Amy once the nativity play was over. How very strange.

Next morning Sister Carter was happy to agree to Emma's request to take the time owing to her that afternoon. In her usual way, she didn't question why Emma should want to take it at such short notice and Emma didn't volunteer the information either. Although Daniel had said that there was no need to keep things a secret, she simply didn't feel comfortable discussing his affairs. However, it soon became obvious that the gossip mongers had been at work.

'Come on, then—give. What were you doing in dishy Daniel's car last night, you dark horse?'

Jane Goodyear followed Emma into the kitchen when she went to fetch a fresh jug of water for Shirley Rogers. Shirley was in some discomfort that morning and they were waiting for Max Dennison to arrive and examine her. Consequently, Emma was a little distracted and not quite as quick as she might have been in thinking up an excuse.

'I…um…I was doing him a favour,' she muttered, picking up the jug and hurriedly making her way back to the door.

'Oh, I see.' Jane's tone was teasing. 'I wonder what sort of favour.' She glanced round as Linda walked past the door. 'Did you know that Emma here has been doing Daniel Hutton *favours?*'

'I certainly didn't! You sly thing, Emma Graham. I knew you were up to something last night! Now, come on—'

'If you could spare the time, Staff, I'd like to check on Paula Walters.'

Daniel's tone was so dry that Emma felt her face go red. Had he overheard what the other two had said? she wondered miserably as she handed the jug to Jane and followed him into the ward. However, there was no way she could ask him in front of a patient so she was forced to hold her tongue.

He greeted Paula in his usual courteous way then sat by the bed and explained that the ultrasound scan had shown several very large fibroids in her uterus. Paula began to cry before he'd got very far.

'I'll have to have a hysterectomy, won't I? That's what you're telling me, Doctor?'

'No.' Daniel smiled when he saw her surprise. 'Mr Dennison and I have talked this over very carefully and decided that we shall opt for a myomectomy. I explained what that was yesterday, if you recall?'

'You said that it meant removing the fibroids from my womb. So that means I shall still be able to have children—is that what you're saying, Dr Hutton?'

'Exactly. Normally we might have opted for a hysterectomy in a case like this. However, in view of your age and the fact that you're hoping to start a family, we shall carry out a myomectomy instead.' He shrugged. 'It will take a little more time but the end results will be worth it, won't they?'

'Oh, yes!' Paula smiled through her tears. 'Oh, I'm so relieved! I can't tell you how worried I was.'

Daniel laughed as he patted her arm. 'I think I can see that for myself. Anyway, we're scheduling the operation for tomorrow morning. As luck would have it, there's a free slot, so the sooner we get it over with, the faster you'll be back to your old self.'

With one last smile, he left Paula's bedside. Emma hurried after him but she didn't get chance to explain what had been going on as just at that point Mr Dennison arrived. It was all systems go after that as the consultant made his rounds in his usual imperious fashion. Mike Humphreys was with him but he cut Emma dead.

Mike was obviously still annoyed, she thought as she went to attend to a patient who was feeling sick after her pre-med. However, there was little she could do about it so she put it out of her mind for the rest of the morning. She was just getting ready to go off duty when Daniel phoned and left a message for her to meet him in the car park.

Linda took the call but mercifully she didn't get a chance to ask any questions as Sister called her away. However,

Emma knew that she would be given the third degree the following day. Still, it couldn't be helped so she would worry about it when she had to and not let it spoil the day. She was looking forward to it so much, and she knew that it wasn't just the thought of watching Amy in the play. Being with Daniel for a whole afternoon made it seem even more special.

He was waiting in his car for her and he opened the door as soon as she appeared. 'I thought we could stop off and have lunch beforehand,' he began, then stopped as his pager beeped. He checked the display and sighed. 'A and E. I'll have to go back in and see what they want.'

Emma stayed in the car, listening to the radio. Daniel came back a few minutes later, looking harried. 'We've had an emergency brought into A and E—an ectopic pregnancy, from the look of it. Max is tied up in a meeting at the moment so I'll have to deal with it. I'm sorry, Emma, but we're going to have to forget about lunch, I'm afraid.'

'Will you be finished in time for Amy's play?' she asked, her own disappointment forgotten as she thought how upset the child would be if Daniel wasn't there to watch her perform.

'I hope so, but I'm not sure how long this will take. The patient is in a pretty bad way, I'm afraid.' Daniel's tone was grim. 'Damn! Of all the times for this to happen. Still, at least you'll be there on time even if I'm late. You don't mind going on your own, do you, Emma? Only Amy will be so upset if there's no one there to watch her.'

'Of course I don't mind! Just tell me where her school is.'

Daniel explained then helped her out of the car. 'I don't know how to thank you for this, Emma. Really, I don't.'

He kissed her quickly on the cheek and his eyes were warm when he straightened. 'You're a real friend!'

Emma sighed as he hurried back inside the hospital. A friend, was she? Maybe she should have been satisfied to hear that but she couldn't help wishing that Daniel thought of her as more than just a friend, silly though that idea undoubtedly was. It would be nice to know that Daniel considered her to be special…very nice, indeed!

The school hall was packed when Emma arrived a little after two that afternoon. She found a seat near the back and looked around, but she couldn't see any sign of Daniel. Was he still in the operating theatre? She could only assume so.

Emma settled down to enjoy the performance as the curtains parted. There was a lot of shuffling as the children tried to spot their parents amongst the audience. Amy saw her and waved enthusiastically from where she was standing with the rest of the angels at the side of the stage.

Emma waved back, hiding a smile as she saw the little girl's tinsel halo had slipped to one side and was dangling over her right ear. All the angels were wearing the same costume and she was pleased to see that Amy's fitted in perfectly with the others. Mary was wearing a long blue gown with a pyjama cord tied around her waist, while Joseph and the shepherds were sporting what looked suspiciously like check teatowels on their heads. However, any shortcomings in the costumes didn't detract from her enjoyment. There was something very touching about watching the children perform their version of the Christmas story.

'Hi! I didn't think I was going to make it in time.'

Daniel quietly slid into the seat next to hers and Emma smiled at him. 'I'm glad you're here. Amy would have been so disappointed if you'd missed her performance.'

'So would I have been. I've been looking forward to this.' There was a note of pride in Daniel's voice which he didn't attempt to hide. Emma smiled as she realised just how much he loved his small niece. Daniel was making a wonderful job of looking after Amy in very difficult circumstances. She couldn't help thinking how few men would have devoted all their time and energy to bringing up a child, as he was doing. But, then, Daniel was a very special kind of man.

Her heart gave a small hiccup and she frowned, wondering why that thought should have disturbed her so much. However, it really wasn't the time to start worrying about it so she concentrated on the play instead. Nevertheless, she was very aware of Daniel sitting beside her, his large frame crammed onto the too-small chair.

When she breathed in she could smell the spicy fragrance of the soap he'd used, and when he leaned over so that he could get a better view of the three kings as they made their entrance—resplendent in someone's gold brocade curtains—she could feel the warmth of his body passing into hers. Suddenly her senses seemed to be heightened to an incredible degree, leaving her open to all sorts of emotions.

When the children began to sing 'Away in a manger' Emma felt tears start to trickle down her face. There was something so innocent and magical about the shrill little voices singing the beautiful old carol that it touched her heart.

'Here.' Daniel pressed a clean white handkerchief into her hand and his eyes were tender as he looked at her. 'It brings a lump to your throat, doesn't it?'

Emma nodded as she dabbed her eyes. 'It does.'

It seemed the most natural thing in the world after that when Daniel took hold of her hand and kept hold of it throughout the rest of the performance. It just seemed to add to the magic of the occasion. Emma couldn't remember when anything had moved her so much. It made no difference when two of the shepherds had a bit of a scrap because they each wanted to carry the toy lamb or that one of the wise men was so overcome with stage fright that he forgot his lines. The wonder and joy of that first Christmas was to be celebrated and who better to do that than the children?

Everyone clapped enthusiastically when the play ended. The children were very excited as they came racing down from the stage to find their parents. Amy's little face was aglow as she ran up to Emma and Daniel. Her halo was dangling over one ear and her wings looked very much the worse for wear, but it was obvious how delighted she was to have them both there.

'Did you see me? Could you hear me singing?' she demanded, hopping excitedly up and down.

'We could! And you were brilliant, sweetheart!' Daniel bent and hugged her. He exchanged a look with Emma and she smiled back. It was the sort of proudly amused look a lot of parents were exchanging, she thought, then felt her heart leap as it hit her what she was doing. She wasn't Amy's parent, for heaven's sake!

'What's wrong?'

With his usual astuteness, Daniel had homed in on her mood. Emma fixed a bright smile firmly in place, terrified that he might guess what she'd been thinking. It gave her hot and cold chills to imagine what his reaction would be.

'Nothing. What could be wrong after a brilliant performance like that? Well done, Amy. I really enjoyed it.'

'I told everyone you were coming,' Amy declared, catching hold of Emma's hand. 'My teacher and Ruth and Becky—they're my best friends—and the dinner ladies. Everyone! I told them *all* that you'd be here to watch me, Emma.'

'Did you, darling?' Emma was touched her presence should have meant so much to the child. She bent and kissed Amy, earning herself another huge smile. The little girl went racing off as one of her friends called to her just then.

'Thank you for sparing the time to come today, Emma. Having you here has made it all the more special for Amy.'

There was a pensive note in Daniel's voice. Emma frowned as she wondered what had caused it. However,

Amy came back at that moment so there was no opportunity to ask him. Amy insisted on leaving her costume on to go home in. Daniel had his car outside and they left the school together.

Emma hung back as he unlocked the car doors. She couldn't help feeling a little down at the thought that now the play was over Daniel would no longer need her help.

'Well, I'll see you both soon, I hope,' she said in a determinedly bright voice. 'And thank you again for asking me to watch your play, Amy. It was wonderful.'

'You aren't in a rush, are you?' Daniel asked as he turned to her. 'I was hoping that you'd come back and have tea with us.'

'Yes! Will you, Emma...please, please, please?' Amy added her invitation to Daniel's, making it hard for Emma to refuse, but she knew that it was foolish to delay the inevitable any longer.

'It's very kind of you both but I'm sure you don't really want me having tea with you *again*.' She laughed, making a joke of it because her heart was aching at the thought of this being the end of the road for the three of them. Maybe it was silly but she couldn't recall enjoying herself as much as she had these past two days, being a part of Daniel's and Amy's lives.

'Course we do! Don't we, Uncle Daniel?' Amy turned beseechingly to her uncle. Emma saw him frown and quickly stepped in. She didn't want Daniel being forced into doing something he didn't want to do out of politeness.

'No, really. I'm sure you must have a lot of things to do,' she began, but he shook his head.

'Nothing that can't wait.' He glanced at his niece and his face softened. 'Amy will be very disappointed if you don't help us celebrate her success, Emma.'

'Well...' Emma found herself wavering. What harm could there be in spending another couple of hours with Daniel and Amy? a small voice whispered seductively.

'That's settled, then. Good!' Daniel immediately took advantage of her hesitation. Whisking open the car door, he stepped back and bowed. 'Your carriage awaits you, ma'am!'

Emma shook her head. 'I give in. I can tell that I won't win.' She slid into the seat, smiling up at Daniel as he started to close the door. 'You can be very persuasive when you set your mind to it, Dr Hutton.'

'I try my best.' His hazel eyes sparkled with laughter as they held hers for a moment before he closed the door. Emma sank back in the seat, making a great performance out of fastening her seat belt as he got into the car. She took a deep breath but she could feel her insides wobbling. Did Daniel have any idea what he did to a woman's equilibrium when he looked at her like that?

She shot a sideways glance at him as he started the car, and sighed. He must have! He couldn't have got to this stage in his life and remained unaware of the effect he had on the opposite sex.

It was a sobering thought when she definitely needed sobering. To imagine that the look Daniel had given her had been meant only for her would be a mistake. Daniel wasn't at all interested in her in *that* way!

In the end they went to Emma's flat. She'd felt guilty about letting Daniel cook again so she'd offered to make them a meal. Daniel and Amy had been only too eager to agree to the suggestion and had made short work of the home-made cottage pie she'd taken from her small freezer and cooked for them. Now Amy was kneeling by the coffee-table, writing a letter to Father Christmas, while Emma and Daniel drank coffee.

'I like what you've done in here,' he said approvingly, looking around the room. 'That colour on the walls is beautiful and those stencils are wonderful. You must have a lot of patience!'

'Thank you.' Emma smiled as she looked at the warm, terracotta-coloured walls and the intricate border she'd stencilled so painstakingly around them. 'I have to admit that halfway through decorating this room I wondered if I'd taken leave of my senses. I was up a ladder at the time, trying to reach the ceiling and wishing that my arms were at least six inches longer. I don't think I would have been half as ambitious if I'd realised what hard work it would be!'

'But it was worth it, believe me. If you ever want to change careers then I have a house which is in serious need of decorating,' Daniel began.

'No way!' Emma held up her hands. 'I shall stick to nursing, thank you. It may be hard work but it beats being up a twenty-foot ladder any day of the week. And talking of work, how did you get on with that emergency ectopic?'

Daniel grimaced. 'It was pretty scary, I can tell you. The tube had ruptured so I had to remove it and she'd lost a lot of blood. Hopefully, we caught it in time but she's gone to ICU just to be on the safe side.'

'Fingers crossed, then,' Emma said quietly. Ectopic pregnancies—where a foetus developed outside the uterus—were always dangerous. Most were discovered within the first two months after conception but a few went undetected until they gave real cause for concern.

They let the subject drop as Amy looked up just then. 'Do you know where Father Christmas lives, Uncle Daniel? Mummy used to know 'cos she always posted my letters to him.'

'I think he lives at the North Pole,' Daniel replied seriously. 'I shall have to see if I can find his address.'

'Mummy had a book with addresses in,' Amy said at once. 'Maybe she wrote it down in there.'

'I'm sure she did. Your mummy was very clever about remembering to do things like that.' There was a catch in Daniel's voice as he said that. Emma sighed to herself as she realised that he still missed his sister a lot. It couldn't have been easy for him, coping with his own grief over Claire's death and having to keep up a front for Amy's sake.

Thankfully, Amy didn't appear to have noticed anything amiss. She got up and came over to them. 'Would you like to see my letter? It isn't a secret. Mummy said that Father Christmas didn't mind if mummies and daddies read the letters first,' she explained. 'So I'm sure he won't mind if you read it, Uncle Daniel.'

'Thank you, sweetheart.' Daniel took the letter from his niece and quickly read it. Emma was watching and she saw him tense. It made her wonder what the child had asked for.

Daniel cleared his throat but Emma could tell that he was having trouble controlling his emotions. 'That's a lovely letter, Amy,' he said quietly, although his voice grated.

Emma decided that he needed a moment to collect himself so she quickly turned to the little girl. 'If you go into the kitchen and look in the dresser drawer, you'll find a packet of envelopes, Amy. I have some stamps as well so you'll be able to post your letter to Father Christmas in the morning on your way to school.'

'Yes!'

Amy went rushing out of the room and they could hear her racing along the hall to the kitchen. Daniel took a deep breath as he ran a hand over his face.

'Thanks, Emma. I could feel myself getting a bit choked up and the last thing I want is to upset Amy. Take a look at what she's written and you'll understand why.'

Emma took the letter from him and read what the little girl had written in her best handwriting. She felt her own eyes mist with tears before she had got to the bottom of the page.

Dear Father Christmas,

My mummy has gone to heaven and I miss her a lot. My Uncle Daniel is looking after me now and he is very nice. I love him loads. I don't want lots of presents this year 'cept a Barbie doll with a sparkly dress. I just want Christmas to be special like it was when Mummy was here. We used to have a big tree with lots of lights and Mummy made mince pies and took me carol singing.

I don't know if you can make things like that happen but will you try.

Lots of love,

Amy Louise Hutton.

XXXXX

P.S. Please give Rudolph a big kiss from me.

'I don't know what to say, Daniel.' Emma took a tissue from her pocket and wiped her eyes. 'It doesn't seem a lot to ask, does it? All Amy wants is a really special Christmas, like all the other Christmases she's had.'

'I know.' Daniel stood up abruptly and went to the window. His back was rigid as he stood there, looking out. Emma ached to find the right words to comfort him but what could she say in a situation like this?

Daniel swung round and his face was filled with determination all of a sudden. 'If that's what Amy wants then that's what she's going to have. I'm going to make sure that child has a Christmas she will always remember, but I can't do it all by myself.'

He crossed the room in a couple of long strides and drew Emma to her feet. 'Will you help me, Emma? Will you help me make a little girl's dreams come true?'

CHAPTER FIVE

'ME? OH, but I'm not sure if I can.'

Emma saw Daniel's eyes darken. 'Why not? It's obvious how much Amy likes you...' He broke off and a look of chagrin crossed his face as he let go of her hands.

'Sorry. Of course, you already have plans for Christmas and you'll be far too busy to help me. I'm sorry, Emma, I shouldn't have put you on the spot like that. Forget I said anything.'

He picked up his coat from the back of the sofa and smiled politely at her. 'Thanks for the meal and for coming to watch Amy today. We both appreciated it.'

'It was my pleasure.' Emma knew she could leave it at that and Daniel wouldn't think any the worse of her. However, innate honesty refused to let him leave without telling him the truth.

'About what you said just now, well, you were wrong.' She hurried on when he looked quizzically at her. 'I don't have any plans for Christmas, to be honest.'

'You don't? Then why did you say that you couldn't help me?' He paused. 'There I go again. Maybe you simply don't want to get involved in this, Emma. That's up to you, of course.'

'Oh, but I *do!* I would love to help you give Amy a wonderful Christmas.' She saw his surprise and looked away in case her expression was too revealing. Would Daniel guess just how much the idea appealed to her? she wondered.

'I'm just not sure if I'm the right person to ask, you see,' she mumbled, disturbed by the thought. Why should the thought of spending more time with him make her heart sing? It didn't make sense.

'Why ever not?'

She could hear the bewilderment in his voice and bit back a sigh. However, now that she'd started, she had to explain.

'Because I've never had the sort of Christmas Amy expects. I have no idea what a real family Christmas should be like, actually. I usually spend Christmas day on my own if I'm not working.'

'Didn't you celebrate Christmas when you were in the children's home?' Daniel asked softly.

Emma shrugged. 'Yes, but it wasn't the same as spending Christmas with your family. The staff used to work split shifts and worked either morning, afternoon or evening. I always got the impression that they would have preferred to be at home with their own families rather than with us.'

'Then it's even more important that we make this year special.' Daniel came back across the room and his eyes seemed to blaze as he looked at her. 'For you, Emma, as well as for Amy!'

Emma looked away because she wasn't proof against the concern she saw on his face. Obviously, Daniel meant what he said and she appreciated it. However, she couldn't help thinking how hard it was going to be once Christmas was over and everything went back to normal again. Was it really wise to let herself get more deeply involved in his life when there could be no future in it?

Amy came back with the envelope just then so the subject was dropped. Emma helped the child address her letter to Father Christmas and found her a stamp. Daniel promised that he would check to make sure the address was correct as soon as they got home.

It was gone seven by that time and Emma knew that he must be anxious to take Amy home and put her to bed, so she didn't delay them. She accompanied them down the four flights of stairs to the ground floor, shivering as an icy wind whipped into the hall when she opened the front door.

Daniel quickly ushered his niece out to his car and got her settled then ran back to say goodbye. 'You look half-frozen, Emma, so I won't keep you standing there too long. I just want to say thanks once again for everything you've done and ask you to promise me that you'll think about spending Christmas with us.'

Emma smiled at him. 'You don't give up easily, do you?'

He laughed at that. 'Nope!'

He sobered abruptly and his eyes held an expression she found it impossible to define as he looked at her. 'I really hope you'll agree, Emma. I can't think of anything I'd enjoy more than the three of us spending Christmas together this year.'

He brushed her mouth with a kiss that was too fleeting to be more than a token. Emma watched as he ran back to his car and got in. He hooted then drove away.

Emma shut the door and went back upstairs, thinking about what had happened. Daniel had kissed her out of gratitude, of course. He'd been grateful for her help in making Amy's costume and he'd appreciated her going to watch his niece in the nativity play. He'd also wanted to thank her for providing them with their tea...

She sighed as she realised that she was listing all the reasons Daniel should have kissed her because it was the only way to stop her foolish mind running away with itself! Why bother?

She spent the rest of the evening weaving seductive little scenarios in which Daniel kissed her for a whole lot of *different* reasons...

'Paula Walters is first on this morning's list. Linda is just sorting out the paperwork.'

It was early on Friday morning and Emma had arrived to find that it was going to be another busy day. Sister

Carter was running through the schedule and it was hectic even by their standards.

'Shirley Rogers is going to be with us a bit longer than expected, I'm afraid,' Sister continued. 'Her temperature is still higher than it should be and Mr Dennison is worried about infection. I want you to keep an eye on her, Emma. I think hourly obs would be best until we see what's happening.'

'Of course, Sister,' Emma agreed, hoping that the problem would resolve itself given time and the appropriate treatment. Although strict controls were used during surgery, there were odd occasions when infection could set in. Hopefully, this setback would be only a temporary one in Shirley's case.

Once Sister Carter had finished going through her list, Emma went to check on Shirley. She found her looking rather dispirited that day, although in her usual way Shirley did her best to make light of what had happened.

'Seems you might have to put up with me a bit longer, love,' Shirley told her as Emma reached for the thermometer.

'So I believe. I don't know how we're going to stand all the moaning you do,' Emma teased, popping the thermometer under Shirley's tongue.

Shirley gurgled, hampered by the thermometer sticking out of her mouth. 'Wait till my hubby hears that he's got to put up with a few more days of his own cooking. He will be pleased—I don't think!'

'It will make him appreciate you all the more, won't it?' Emma replied with a laugh. She jotted the reading down on Shirley's chart. 'So how do you feel in general?'

'Oh, you know…as though one of our bulls has trampled me.' Shirley laid her hand on her stomach and winced. 'It's a bit painful where the stitches are, to be honest, love.'

'Let me take a look,' Emma offered immediately. She frowned when she saw how swollen the skin either side of the sutures looked. 'I think I'll ask Dr Hutton to take a look at that. He should be up in a moment to see Mrs Walters.'

'Whatever you think best, love,' Shirley agreed in her usual co-operative way. Emma couldn't help wishing that they had more patients like Shirley Rogers. Life would be so much easier then!

Afternoon came round and it was Emma's turn to work in the outpatients' clinic that day. Daniel was the doctor in attendance and he was already in his consulting room when Emma arrived after lunch.

She tapped on the door and went in, smiling as he looked up from the notes he'd been writing. Although she'd seen him in passing on the ward that morning, this was the first real opportunity she'd had to speak to him. She couldn't deny that her spirits seemed to lift at the thought of the next couple of hours they would spend together.

'From the look of the queue out there, it's going to be a busy session,' she announced cheerfully.

'As usual!' he replied dryly, tossing down his pen. He sat back in his chair and regarded her levelly. 'So, have you made up your mind yet?'

Emma didn't pretend that she hadn't understood. 'About Christmas? Yes, I have.' She took a quick breath, hoping that she wasn't making a mistake. She'd thought hard about what her decision should be, but at the end of the day she'd known in her heart that she couldn't bear to think of letting Amy down. 'If you want me to help you then I shall.'

'Great!' Daniel got up and came round the desk. He gave her a quick hug then let her go when there was a knock on the door. Smoothing his face into its customary expression, he bade the receptionist—who had brought the patients' files—to come in. However, Emma had seen enough to know how delighted he was by her decision.

She smiled to herself as she went to summon the first patient on the list. Obviously, Daniel was pleased because it would take some of the pressure off him, having her to help him get everything ready. However, she couldn't help hoping that he'd been pleased because it was *she* who would be working with him to give Amy a wonderful Christmas. For some reason that seemed more important than anything else.

'So, Mrs Dyson, how have you been since we last saw you?'

Daniel smiled at the elderly lady seated in front of the desk. Emily Dyson was a woman in her late sixties, a widow who had three grown-up children. She'd been referred by her GP a few months earlier when he'd noticed that she'd had a slight prolapse of the uterus.

An appointment had been made at the clinic and she'd seen Max Dennison, who'd recommended a ring pessary to hold the uterus in position. Unfortunately, the pessary had caused stress incontinence, which Mrs Dyson had mentioned at her second visit. A larger pessary had been fitted and today's appointment was to monitor the situation.

'Worse than ever, I'm afraid, Doctor.' Emily Dyson sighed wearily. 'The incontinence problem is really getting me down now. It's so embarrassing, you understand.'

'I'm sure it is.' Daniel looked at her notes again. 'To be honest, Mrs Dyson, I think we are heading towards surgery now. It's obvious that the pessaries aren't working so I really feel that a vaginal hysterectomy and repair would be your best option.'

'If that's what you think would be best, Doctor.'

Emma frowned as she heard the dispirited note in the elderly lady's voice. It was obvious that Mrs Dyson wasn't altogether happy with the thought of having an operation, even though she'd agreed with Daniel.

Daniel obviously had noticed it as well because he frowned. 'You don't sound too keen on the idea, Mrs Dyson. Why is that?'

'Well, it just seems as though things have all sort of

snowballed.' Emily Dyson clutched her bag. It was obvious that she felt uncomfortable about saying anything. However, Daniel urged her on, smiling to put her at ease.

'That sounds very intriguing! You can't possibly leave it like that and not explain what you meant.'

The elderly lady smiled and once again Emma thought how good he was with people. Daniel really cared about them as individuals, not just as *patients*. It just served to increase her admiration for him.

'I suppose I'd better, although I've not liked to say anything before, you understand. I know all the doctors I've seen have told me that I have a prolapse but it never caused me a bit of bother. I didn't know there was anything wrong until my GP mentioned it,' she explained.

'So that wasn't the reason why you visited your GP in the first place?' Daniel queried.

'Oh, no! I just went for a smear, you see. I'd never had one before—never seen the need, to be honest. But my daughter, Betty, well, she'd been on and on at me to go so I did. It was then that my GP discovered that I had a problem, although I'd had no idea that there was anything wrong up till then.'

'I see.' Daniel frowned. 'And the incontinence problem? When did that first crop up?'

'After I had that ring fitted. I'd never had a bit of trouble before that.' Emily Dyson sighed. 'And it's got even worse since they decided I needed a bigger one fitted.'

'And now I'm telling you that you need an operation. I can see why you would be so confused, Mrs Dyson. Here we are telling you that we can solve your problem this way or that when you didn't even *have* a problem to begin with!' Daniel's tone was wry. 'Why didn't you say something sooner?'

'Well, I didn't like to. I mean, it isn't for me to argue with a doctor, is it?'

Emma barely managed to hide her dismay. The poor

soul! Fancy getting swept along in the system because she hadn't felt that she had the right to question what was happening.

'What would you say if I suggested that we went right back to the beginning, Mrs Dyson? We can remove that ring pessary and see how you go from there,' Daniel suggested gently.

'And I won't need an operation?' Emily Dyson's face broke into a relieved smile. 'Oh, that would be lovely, Doctor. Thank you so much!'

It was a very happy woman who left the clinic a short time later. Emma sighed as she watched the old lady walking purposefully down the corridor. 'Incredible, isn't it? That poor woman would have gone through with an operation rather than say, Hang on but I don't want this.'

'It is. But a lot of older people feel the same way—that they can't question what their doctor tells them.' Daniel grimaced. 'I just wish that someone had picked up on the problem—or, rather, lack of one—sooner, instead of putting that poor woman through so much unnecessary worry and discomfort. In some instances it's better to leave well alone rather than try to do anything!'

'That's a lesson we should all learn,' Emma said thoughtfully. 'I shall be a lot more aware of it in future.'

'Oh, I think you're already very quick to pick up on problems,' Daniel observed lightly. 'I could tell that you'd sensed something wasn't quite right with our Mrs Dyson. Nurses like you, Emma, are worth your weight in gold.'

'Try telling that to the management. Maybe they'll give me a pay rise!' she retorted lightly, because the comment had meant such a lot to her.

'I doubt it. They'd be bankrupt if they had to pay all the nursing staff what they're really worth!'

Her pleasure dissipated a little as she realised that he must view all the nursing staff in the same favourable light. However, she shrugged off the feeling of disappointment by telling herself how silly it was. They worked their way through the rest of the list and then it was five o'clock and time to go home.

Emma gathered together the files to take them to the office but paused as Daniel called to her.

'Just before you go, Emma, are you free tomorrow by any chance?'

Emma looked round, trying to quieten the noisy thundering her heart was making. 'Yes, as it happens. It's my long weekend.'

'Great! Then how about making a start on the Christmas preparations?' Daniel picked up his pen and slipped it into the top pocket of his white coat. He accompanied Emma from the room.

'Fine by me. What did you have in mind?'

'It's knowing where to start, isn't it?' He grimaced as he ran his hand through his hair. 'I'm a novice at all this, I'm afraid. If I wasn't working then I used to spend the day with Claire, and if I was working I'd still not need to actually *do* anything. I had Christmas dinner in the staff canteen and simply bought a few presents and left it at that!'

Emma laughed at the rueful note in his voice. 'Snap! We're a right pair, aren't we?'

'Well, at least there are two of us and you know what they say about two heads being better than one.' Daniel's smile was warm and Emma couldn't help smiling back.

'Mmm, I'll reserve judgement on that, thank you! Maybe we should compile a list to make sure that we don't forget anything?' she suggested. 'It would be a start.'

'Good idea! Why didn't I think of it? Mind you, I do know the first thing we need because Amy has been nagging me for days now—a Christmas tree. Why don't we buy that tomorrow then do as you suggested and make a list of everything else that needs doing?'

Emma frowned. She didn't want Daniel to think he had

to ask her to accompany him and Amy everywhere. 'Are you sure you need me to come along?'

'Of course! This is your Christmas as much as it's Amy's and mine.' He sounded so surprised that any reservations she'd had instantly disappeared.

'Very well, then. I'd love to come with you. The only question now is where shall we go for a tree? There are still some left in the shops in town, I expect.'

Daniel shook his head. 'No. The best of them will have been sold by now. We want this tree to be extra-special, don't we? Tell you what, I'll check out the best place to buy a Christmas tree and you just be ready bright and early in the morning. OK?'

'OK,' Emma agreed. Daniel sketched her a wave then hurried off. He was obviously anxious to collect his niece from the childminder's house.

Emma took the files to the office then went back to the ward to collect her coat. Linda and Jane were just leaving and they paused as they saw her stepping from the lift.

'So how did it go? You and Daniel have a nice afternoon together, did you?' Jane asked pertly.

'I don't know about nice but it was busy,' Emma replied noncommittally. She took off her uniform and slipped into her outdoor clothes. Linda and Jane were still waiting and she sighed as she realised that she was going to have to explain what was going on at some point.

'Well, I never! Just imagine, Daniel has been looking after that little girl all by himself and none of us knew a thing about it,' Linda declared after Emma had finished.

'I don't think he wanted it broadcasted, although he did say that he hadn't been deliberately trying to keep it a secret.' Emma shrugged on her coat and headed for the door. 'So don't go spreading it all round the place, you two.'

'Oh, you can trust us, Emma!' Linda claimed, looking hurt. 'Anyway, it does explain why you weren't too worried about falling out with Mike. You have bigger—and better—fish to fry!'

'It isn't like that! I'm just helping Daniel out over Christmas,' she declared. 'There isn't anything, well, *romantic* about the situation.'

'Come on! This is me you're talking to, kiddo.' Linda placed a friendly arm around Emma's shoulders and winked at Jane. 'You can tell us till you're blue in the face that you're only doing this for the most altruistic reasons, but I won't believe you. No woman worth her salt is immune to Dr Delectable Hutton!'

Emma sighed as Linda and Jane both laughed. She knew that it was pointless, trying to convince them they were wrong. It would have been a lie anyway, she acknowledged as they all walked to the lift together. She wasn't helping Daniel *only* for Amy's sake, but for her own as well. Prolonging the time she could spend with him was part of the attraction...

Saturday was cold and windy but mercifully dry. When Emma left her flat just before eight to buy some milk, she was glad that she'd dressed in her warmest clothes. Across the road, the waves were bouncing against the breakwaters, sending up plumes of spray which sparkled in the frosty air. It would be high tide that night, and if the wind kept up there was a very real danger that some parts of the coastline might be flooded. There had been a lot of erosion in the area and the local council had been trying to get government funding to repair the damage. Only last winter a house had fallen into the sea when a section of the cliff face had broken away.

Emma hurried home with her pint of milk and made coffee and toast which she ate standing by the window. Daniel hadn't said what time he would be coming for her and she didn't want to miss him. It was barely eight-thirty when she saw his car pulling up and she waved as she saw him looking up at her window.

Emma hurriedly collected her bag, shooting a glance in the mirror as she passed it to check her appearance. She'd decided on denim jeans and a chunky blue sweater which made her grey eyes appear even greyer by contrast. The sweater had a roll neck which would keep out the chill and it went well with her padded jacket which was a deeper shade of blue.

She'd brushed her short hair until it gleamed like spun gold as it curled around her heart-shaped face. Her make-up consisted of a lot of moisturiser to protect her skin, a little mascara and a slick of pale bronze lipstick. However, she felt quite pleased with the overall effect, if she was honest. Daniel shouldn't be ashamed to be seen with her at least...

She cut short that silly thought and quickly ran down the stairs. This outing wasn't a date! It was simply a first step towards making sure that Amy had a wonderful Christmas. However, it was impossible to curb the way her heart lifted when Daniel leaned over to open the door for her.

'Hi, there. I was hoping it wasn't too early to collect you but someone—naming no names, of course—couldn't wait any longer!'

He shot a meaningful glance in the rear-view mirror and Emma laughed. 'I wonder if I can guess who that someone is?' She turned and smiled at the little girl strapped into the back seat.

'Are you excited about choosing your tree, Amy?'

'Yes! I told Uncle Daniel that you wouldn't mind what time we came for you. You don't, do you, Emma?' the child asked uncertainly.

Emma smiled at her. 'Of course not! I'm looking forward to it.' She turned to Daniel and in her haughtiest tone in- structed, 'Get a move on, my good man. We have a tree to buy. Don't spare the horses!'

'Yes, ma'am!' Daniel treated her to a mocking salute then started the car. Emma sank back in the seat, smiling to herself. It felt so good to be able to tease him like that, so *right*. It made her wonder what it would feel like to be able to do it on a permanent basis.

She sighed. Sometimes it was better not to wish for too much. That way you didn't run the risk of being disappointed.

'Amy, are you sure that's the one you really want?'

Daniel's tone was tinged with disbelief as he studied the scrawny little Christmas tree his niece was pointing to. He'd brought them to a garden centre several miles outside the town. The place was obviously extremely popular because the car park had been packed when they'd arrived. Daniel had managed to find them a space then, at Amy's insistence, they'd headed straight to where the trees where being sold.

Emma had been amazed by the number of spruce trees which were piled up in the enclosure. There were many different varieties as well, making it even harder to choose. However, Amy had taken one look at the wilting little tree with its twisted branches, standing on its own in a corner, and had made up her mind.

'Yes, that one,' she insisted. 'It looks so sad and lonely, Uncle Daniel. We have to buy it and take it home with us.'

'I don't believe this. What do you say, Emma?' He turned imploringly to her. 'After all, this tree is supposed to be for all of us.'

Emma exchanged a conspiratorial smile with Amy and tried not to laugh. 'Well, if we don't buy it then I'm sure nobody else will.'

'I give up! I can't win, can I? It's two against one.' Daniel shook his head but Emma could tell that he wasn't the least bit annoyed. He paid for the tree and dryly asked the young assistant if he would put it to one side while they went into the shop to buy some decorations. Amy went racing on ahead while Emma and Daniel followed at a more sedate pace.

'Well, I don't think we need worry that anyone will try to gazump us and buy that tree while we're gone,' he said drolly. 'Did you see that boy's face when I told him which tree I wanted? He obviously thought I'd taken leave of my senses!'

Emma laughed. 'Maybe he thought you had poor eyesight and couldn't see the gaps where branches are missing.'

'Don't! Can you imagine how much tinsel it's going to take to make that tree look halfway respectable?' Daniel shook his head in despair. 'Why did Amy have to choose *that* one?'

'Because she has a kind heart, like her uncle,' Emma teased, and earned herself a rueful look.

'Remind me to make some changes to my attitude, will you?' he replied, opening the door for her. 'There's being kind and being *kind!*'

The next couple of hours passed so quickly that Emma could hardly believe it when she saw what time it was. Sitting in the garden centre's bustling café with a steaming mug of hot chocolate in her hands, she realised that she'd never had so much fun as she'd had that morning.

They'd filled numerous carrier bags with decorations, which ranged from the tasteful to the downright hideous, but they'd had a wonderful time. Now Amy had gone to watch the animated display which had been set up in a corner, a moving tableau of elves and fairies helping a harassed-looking Santa.

Daniel took an appreciative swallow of his drink. 'Oh, boy, do I need this! I had no idea that shopping could be so tiring.'

'You've obviously led a charmed life,' Emma teased. 'Anyway, we've just about finished now, haven't we?'

'I hope 'so.' Daniel picked up one of the carriers and poked around inside it. 'Have you see some of this stuff? I hope you weren't expecting an elegant Christmas tree, Emma, one of those done in a few tasteful colours.'

He withdrew a thick coil of purple tinsel from the bag and draped it around her neck then added another in a particularly virulent shade of red. 'Mmm, it's going to be different, I can say that for it.'

'It will be lovely,' Emma declared firmly. 'And I hate those designer-done trees. Who wants only silver decorations on their tree when they can have all these lovely colours, anyway?'

'You're as bad as Amy! Am I the only one with any taste around here?'

Emma laughed as she took the tinsel from around her neck and threw it at him. 'Cheek! Just you wait and see, Daniel Hutton. This tree will be a positive work of art after we've finished with it.'

'From the Picasso school, no doubt,' Daniel retorted as he fielded the tinsel. He put it back in the bag then leaned towards her. 'You've got tinsel in your hair now.'

'Have I?' Emma raised her hand to her head but Daniel got there before her. She felt his fingers gently plucking the glittering strands out of her hair and her breath caught.

'That's it... Oops, no. There's another bit.' He bent closer as he spotted another strand of tinsel. Emma felt as though her lungs were going to burst at any moment. She wanted to breathe out and then breathe in, to act naturally, but it seemed to be beyond her to do that when Daniel was so close to her.

Perhaps her tension communicated itself to him because he suddenly glanced down. His hazel eyes met hers and she couldn't have done anything to stop what happened next even if she'd wanted to.

'Emma...'

Her name was the merest whisper on his lips before they

found hers. His mouth was warm and gentle yet it held a hunger she'd never expected. Daniel kissed her not just because the moment was right and the opportunity was there but because he wanted to. Knowing that, it made her heart lift with joy.

He drew back and smiled at her. 'That's better.'

'Better...' she repeated huskily.

'All the tinsel has gone now.' His hand brushed over her hair one last time before he picked up his cup. However, Emma could see that his hand was trembling when he raised it to his lips.

She looked away, afraid of what might be on her face at that moment. That Daniel had been as affected by that kiss as she had been made her feel more mixed up than ever. Had he asked her to help him just because he wanted to give Amy a marvellous Christmas? Or had there been another reason?

It was impossible to know what the answer was without asking him and she couldn't bring herself to do that. It was something of a relief when Amy came back. Whilst she was concentrating on the little girl there was no room to start wondering about matters which might be best left alone.

They left the garden centre not long after that, stowing the decorations in the boot and fastening the tree securely to the roof-rack. Amy was obviously tired out by all the excitement and quickly dozed off in the back of the car. Daniel put a tape into the stereo and Emma let her mind drift as she listened to a selection of light classics. It was better not to think too hard about what had happened. That way she wouldn't be disappointed if she'd misread the situation.

It was already growing dark when they drew up in front of Daniel's house. The wind was even stronger now, making it difficult to stand upright when they got out of the car. Daniel handed Emma his keys.

'You and Amy go inside and I'll bring in the tree.'

Emma took tight hold of the child's hand as a sudden blast of wind threatened to blow her over. 'Are you sure you can manage?'

'Quite sure,' he replied firmly.

Emma hurried up the path and unlocked the front door. Amy went to take off her coat but Emma waited by the door. She grabbed hold of the tree when the wind caught it as Daniel tried to manoeuvre it through the door.

'Thanks. Looks like we're in for a real storm, doesn't it?' He carried the tree into the living room and propped it up in the corner of the room then went back outside for the bags of decorations.

Emma frowned as she watched him struggling to close the boot. The storm was getting worse and she couldn't help wondering how she would get home later. She didn't want Daniel having to drive her home in the middle of a gale.

By the time he came back inside, she'd made up her mind. 'Look, Daniel, I think I should get off home now. This storm is going to get really bad soon and I don't want to end up stranded.'

'Nonsense! You can't leave now. We have a tree to trim, remember?'

Emma shook her head. 'You and Amy can manage perfectly well without me. It's better that I go now. I don't want you having to drive me home later. I wouldn't have a minute's peace, worrying about you two being out on the roads in weather like this.'

'And I wouldn't have any peace, thinking about you taking the bus.' Daniel folded his arms. 'If the storm gets that bad then there's an easy solution, Emma. You can stay here.'

CHAPTER SIX

'HERE?' Emma echoed.

'Uh-huh. There's a spare bedroom so it isn't as though we don't have enough room. Anyway, you could treat it as a practice run, couldn't you?'

Emma was having trouble following what Daniel was saying. Her brain seemed to have stalled on the thought of staying the night under his roof and wouldn't oblige her by moving forward from that. She ended up by once again repeating what he'd said, and inwardly groaned as she realised that he must think her a complete idiot!

'Practice run?'

'Yes.' He frowned as he looked at her. 'Obviously, you'll be staying here on Christmas Eve, Emma.'

It may have been obvious to him. However, it most certainly hadn't been obvious to her. Emma took a deep breath, but before she could explain that she hadn't thought about it Amy came racing back down the stairs.

'Can we start decorating the tree now, Uncle Daniel?' she demanded eagerly.

Daniel smiled as he turned to his niece. 'Of course we can! You take that stand into the living room and we'll get the tree safely set up before we do anything else.'

'Yes!' Amy picked up the metal supporting stand which they'd bought at the garden centre and carried it into the living room. She set it down in the centre of the room then looked around. 'Here? Then we can see it properly.'

Daniel treated Emma to an amused look and she forced her thoughts into some semblance of order. It would serve no purpose, creating a fuss. She would simply tell Daniel that she didn't think it was a good idea if she stayed at his house on Christmas Eve, although what reason she could give was open to question. She just knew in her heart that it wouldn't be wise.

'Maybe we should put the tree nearer to the window,' Daniel suggested tactfully. 'That way everyone will be able to see it when they walk past the house.'

Amy nodded solemnly. 'Then if they haven't got a lovely tree like ours they can still feel Christmassy?'

'Exactly!' Daniel gave his niece a hug then moved the stand closer to the window. 'Right, now that we've decided where to put it we can make a start. Can you unpack the bags, please, Amy, while I fix up the tree?'

Amy happily began to unload the carrier bags, arranging each item carefully on the sofa. Emma shook her head in amazement as she saw the amount of decorations. 'I didn't realise that we'd bought so much.'

Daniel grinned as he picked up the little tree. 'Think it will hold all that lot?' he teased. 'Maybe you two are starting to wish that you'd bought a proper tree?'

Emma and Amy looked at one another then shook their heads. 'No way!' Emma stated firmly.

'This is going to be the best tree ever, Uncle Daniel!' Amy declared. 'You'll see!'

Daniel rolled his eyes. 'I give up!'

'Right, stand back, you two. Here we go!'

Emma held her breath as Daniel slid the plug into its socket. They had spent a couple of hours trimming the tree and its puny branches were sagging under the weight of all the baubles. They had left testing the lights until the very last moment and now it was time to see if they worked.

'Wait a minute, Uncle Daniel!' Amy raced across the room and turned off the central light, plunging the room into darkness. 'Now you can switch it on.'

'Oh, how lovely!' Emma exclaimed in delight as Daniel flicked the switch and the fairy lights came on. They'd decided on a set of tiny white lights and she thought how lovely they looked, shimmering amongst the branches like miniature stars.

'It really is the best tree ever!' Amy's small face was filled with wonder as she stared at the tree. 'Emma and I told you it would be beautiful, didn't we? And it is!'

Daniel laughed as he put his arms around his niece and hugged her. 'You did, sweetheart. I shouldn't have been such a doubting Thomas, should I?'

'Who's Thomas?' Amy asked, frowning up at him.

'It's just a rather silly saying, poppet,' Daniel explained, exchanging a wry look with Emma. 'It means that I should have believed you two when you told me that this tree was going to look wonderful. I shouldn't have had any doubts.'

'It's all right, Uncle Daniel,' Amy said generously. 'Emma and I don't mind. It's 'cos you're a boy and boys don't know about things like that, you see.'

Daniel laughed. 'Obviously not! Anyway, let's get this mess cleared up then we can have something to eat. Have you seen what time it is?'

He grimaced as he checked his watch. Emma was surprised when she realised how late it was. She'd been having so much fun that she'd lost track of the time. She was just about to suggest that it was time she left when Daniel spoke.

'If you'd mind Amy, I can pop out and buy some fish and chips, Emma.'

'Fish and chips?' Amy clapped her hands in delight and Emma didn't have the heart to refuse and spoil the treat. However, she made up her mind that she would leave as soon as they'd eaten the meal. She and Amy cleared up all the wrappings from the tree decorations while Daniel went to get their supper. They had the table set by the time he came back.

'I just heard on the car radio that there's been a flood warning. Evidently, they're expecting the sea to breach its defences because of this storm,' he informed her as he took off his coat.

'I did wonder if it might happen,' Emma replied, quickly unpacking the steaming hot fish and chips and arranging them on the plates. 'It's high tide tonight as well, you see, so that could cause extra problems.'

'Then why don't you stay here? There doesn't seem any point in taking unnecessary risks.' He frowned. 'Heaven only knows what the roads will be like in a couple of hours' time.'

'You can sleep in my room if you want to, Emma,' Amy told her quickly. 'Then if you get scared by the storm we can snuggle up in bed together. Mummy used to let me snuggle up with her if I was scared.'

Emma's heart ached at the wistful note she'd heard in Amy's voice. It was obvious that Amy still missed her mother a lot. 'Thank you, sweetheart. That's very kind of you but I think it would be better if I went home. I've a lot of things to do in the morning, you see.'

'Oh. All right, then.'

Thankfully, Amy didn't sound too disappointed as she started to eat her supper. However, when Emma glanced at Daniel she could see the pain in his eyes. She knew that he must be thinking about his sister, and her heart went out to him.

Without stopping to think, she touched his hand. He smiled as he gave her fingers a gentle squeeze. It was a moment of sadness made bearable because they'd shared it. It made Emma feel very close to him, closer than she'd felt to anyone ever before.

'So the two little elves stayed at the North Pole and helped Santa make all the presents for the children.'

Emma closed the book and quietly turned off the bedside lamp. Amy had begged Emma to read her a bedtime story before she left and she hadn't been able to refuse the child's pleas. One story had led to another but Amy had finally fallen asleep.

After tucking the quilt around the little girl, Emma crept from the room and went downstairs. It was almost nine and way past the time she should have left. She went to find Daniel to ask him if she could ring for a taxi and discovered that he was in the living room. He'd turned off the light so that the room was lit only by the fairy lights on the Christmas tree.

'Is she asleep at last?' Daniel must have heard her coming downstairs because he turned towards the door. Emma couldn't help thinking how handsome he looked in the soft glow from the tree lights. It was warm in the house so he'd shed his sweater and was wearing only a thin white polo shirt. When he stood up she felt her heart bump heavily as she saw how it clung to his powerful torso, emphasising the perfect conformation of muscles.

'Yes.' She heard the thickness in her voice and cleared her throat. 'It took three stories before she gave in, though.'

Daniel laughed softly. 'I should have warned you that Amy would have you reading until you were hoarse if you let her. In fact, you sound as though your throat is a bit dry, so how about a glass of wine to lubricate it?'

'I...I was just going to ask if I could phone for a taxi, actually.' Emma was glad of the darkness because it hid her blush. Obviously, Daniel had heard that husky note in her voice but mercifully put his own interpretation on its cause.

'Another few minutes won't make much difference surely? And it isn't that late. You should be home by ten even if you stay for a glass of wine.'

Emma laughed at the unashamedly wheedling note in his voice and it helped dispel the tension. 'All right, then. But just one glass and I really must go home.'

'Just one glass it is. Scout's honour!'

He gave her a smiling salute as he left the room. Emma

went and sat on the sofa, resting her head on the cushions. It was so quiet in the room after all the bustle of the day that she found herself sinking deeper into the cushions. She could hear Daniel moving about in the kitchen but the sound was too muted to disturb her…

She jolted awake as she felt her eyelids drooping. Whether it was because of the warmth in the room or the fact that they hadn't stopped all day long, she could barely stay awake. When Daniel came back a few minutes later with the wine she had to force her eyes open once again.

'Sorry it took so long. The wretched cork broke…' He stopped and looked at her. 'Were you asleep?' he asked silkily.

'Um, no, of course not.' Emma sat up straighter and tried to look suitably alert. However, the effect was somewhat spoilt when she felt an enormous yawn creeping up on her.

Daniel laughed as he handed her one of the glasses. 'I believe you although thousands wouldn't! Just try to stay awake long enough to drink that wine. I hope you like white, by the way, because that's all I've got.'

'It's fine. Thank you.' Emma took a sip of the wine while he filled a second glass for himself. He sat down beside her and she flinched as she felt his thigh brush hers.

Burying her face in the glass, she took another swallow of the wine while she tried to control the rush of sensations which had assailed her. It wasn't easy, however. When Daniel bent down to put the bottle on the floor next to the sofa and his arm touched hers, she felt her nerves tauten. Maybe it was the fact that it was dark in the room that made her senses seem hyperactive all of a sudden, but she was so deeply aware of him sitting beside her that it was an effort to behave naturally.

'Not bad, although I can't claim to be an expert.' Daniel smiled at her over the rim of his glass. 'I know if I like a particular wine and that's about it, I'm afraid.'

Emma summoned a smile, pleased that the conversation

had turned to such impersonal topics. If she could concentrate on discussing the relative merits of the wine, she wouldn't be nearly as conscious of him, she reasoned.

'Me, too. Seeing as my budget only stretches to a bottle of whatever is cheapest at the supermarket that week, I don't think I'm going to become an expert either!'

'You mean you don't go in for all that tasting and spitting?' Daniel feigned surprise, making her laugh.

'I most certainly don't! When I buy a bottle of wine I certainly don't waste any of it!'

'Ah, a woman after my own heart.' He grinned at her and Emma couldn't help smiling back. There was a moment when they looked at one another while they shared the joke, and then the mood seemed to shift with a speed that left Emma reeling. She wanted to look away yet she felt incapable of doing that when Daniel's gaze seemed to have mesmerised her.

'Has anyone ever told you how pretty you are, Emma Graham?' he asked softly, his voice grating so that she shivered.

'N-not really,' she muttered. She nervously wet her lips then shivered again when she saw his eyes following the movement of her tongue. Suddenly the atmosphere in the room seemed to crackle as though the air had been charged with electricity. She could feel her body growing tense in response to it, feel the jolt her heart gave when Daniel took the glass from her hand and put it on the floor next to his.

Her grey eyes were enormous as she watched him turn to her once more. She knew that he was going to kiss her and she knew also that he was giving her time to decide if it was what she wanted. Was it? Yes! No! She wasn't sure!

'They must be mad,' he whispered, his warm breath stirring the curls by her ear as he put his arms around her. 'Mad or blind, maybe.'

'Who?' she murmured, struggling to follow what he was saying. It wasn't easy because her brain had so many other things to deal with. Was it wise to let him kiss her? Would she regret it? If only she could decide!

'All those men who haven't told you how beautiful you are, of course.'

Daniel's voice was rich with amusement but there was nothing playful about his kiss. Emma felt the confident way his mouth closed over hers and knew the decision had been taken for her. She closed her eyes and simply gave herself up to the pleasure of being kissed by an expert. It was like a master-class in what a kiss should be, and when it ended she was breathless and shaking. Oddly enough, so was Daniel.

He rested his forehead against hers and his tone was rueful. 'Wow! Did anyone ever tell you what a great kisser you are, Emma Graham?'

'No.' She smiled because the conversation was so ridiculous. 'I'll be getting big-headed if you carry on like this. I'm pretty and a great kisser? Oh, boy!'

He laughed at that. Drawing her into the crook of his arm, he brushed his mouth over the top of her head. 'You're also kind to helpless males and young children.'

'Please!' She grinned up at him, feeling happier than she'd ever felt at that moment. 'I don't know if I can take any more compliments! Anyway, if you were referring to yourself when you mentioned "helpless males" then I think that's exaggerating things a little too much. You don't strike me as at all helpless, Dr Hutton!'

'Maybe not in my professional capacity. However, I'm not sure about in my private life.'

There had been the strangest note in his voice when he'd said that. Emma frowned as a chill ran through her. Had it been a reference to something that had happened in the past? Once again the thought surfaced that Daniel had been in a relationship which had gone wrong. She was on the verge of asking him to explain what he'd meant when the telephone rang.

'I wonder who that can be. I'd better answer it before it wakes Amy.'

Daniel hurried from the room, turning on the main light as he did so. Emma blinked as she looked around the room. Suddenly, the magic which had been in the air a few moments earlier seemed to have disappeared. Why *had* Daniel kissed her just now? Because he was a normal, healthy male, programmed to respond when there was a young and obviously willing female beside him?

The thought was perhaps a little too close to the truth. Emma stood up abruptly, hating herself because it had hurt so much to realise it. It was an effort to hide how she felt when Daniel came back. However, one look at the grim expression on his face told her that there must be something seriously wrong.

'What's happened?' she demanded anxiously.

'That was Max on the phone to tell me that there's been an accident on the outskirts of town. Evidently, the high tide has washed away a section of the coast road and the rescue services aren't sure how many people may have been injured.

'They've managed to rescue six so far but there's every chance that there will be more casualties. The hospital has declared it a major incident and are asking for all staff to report for duty.'

'We'd better get into work, then...' Emma stopped in dismay. 'What about Amy?'

'Max said that if I couldn't find anyone to mind her, I should bring her with me.' Daniel shrugged. 'It isn't ideal to take her but I can't think what else to do. There's nobody I can leave her with at this time of the night and she can't stay here by herself, that's for sure.'

Emma thought rapidly. 'I could make up a bed for her in the office. She would be safe enough in there and I could keep an eye on her to make sure that she doesn't wander off.'

'Would you?' Daniel looked relieved. 'At least I'd know she was in safe hands with you there, Emma. Heaven knows where I'll be needed and I might not get chance to keep checking on her.'

'You don't need to worry, Daniel. I'll take good care of her,' she assured him.

'I know you will.'

His voice was very deep as he said that. Emma wasn't sure if there had been something behind it but there was no time to ask questions. While Daniel woke up Amy and explained what was happening, Emma put together a bag of toys which she thought the little girl might need. It might be noisy in the ward if they were having to admit patients and it was doubtful if Amy would get much sleep.

Still, at least she'd be there to keep a watchful eye on her, Emma thought as she followed Daniel and Amy out to the car. For some reason that seemed very important. Taking care of Daniel's niece was something she was only too pleased to do…for many reasons.

'We've managed to stop the contractions but she's going to need monitoring closely for the next twenty-four hours.'

Daniel's tone was curt but Emma knew that it was because he was worried. She glanced at the young woman who had been sent up to the ward from the casualty department. Maria Carstairs was twenty-two weeks pregnant with her first child. She had been a passenger in one of the vehicles involved in the RTA and had been rushed in by ambulance because she was threatening to miscarry.

Daniel drew Emma aside while one of the night staff got Maria settled. The extra nursing staff had been deployed wherever they were needed most throughout the hospital. Emma had stayed in her own ward as they were expecting the bulk of the admissions. Beds were at a premium so it was a question of finding places for the injured even though they would need to be moved at a later date. It had meant a lot of juggling around but they were coping.

'The ultrasound shows that the baby is still alive so we just have to keep our fingers crossed, basically. I've put her on salbutamol as a uterine muscle relaxant and that seems to have worked.'

'I'll put her down for half-hourly obs,' Emma assured him. 'How is it down in A and E?'

'Pretty grim, but we're getting there. The police seem to think that they've found all the casualties now, which is something to be thankful for.' He looked round and frowned. 'How's Amy been? I can't imagine that she's been asleep with all the comings and goings tonight. I hope she hasn't been a nuisance?'

'Of course not!' Emma laughed. 'When is she ever a nuisance, Daniel? She's been quite happy in the office, drawing a picture.'

'So long as you haven't been tearing your hair out, trying to look after her and work as well.' Daniel sighed. 'I really didn't mean to offload my responsibilities onto you, Emma. You must be regretting the day you took pity on me and agreed to help.'

'Rubbish! I'm only too happy to help any way I can.'

'Really? You aren't just saying that?' There was a note in his voice which told her that her answer was important to him. She couldn't help wondering why he should doubt that she'd been telling him the truth.

'No, I'm not,' she said firmly, knowing that it was neither the time nor the place to start worrying about it. Even now she could hear the lift arriving, undoubtedly bringing yet another patient to the ward. 'I mean it, Daniel. I really enjoy being with Amy.'

And with you, she added silently, only she thought it better not to mention that fact out loud. However, it did appear that he was reassured.

'Thanks. I don't feel so guilty now—' He stopped as his

pager beeped. 'Looks like I'm wanted again. I'll see you later. Wait for me in the foyer when we're given the all-clear so that I can run you home.'

'You don't need to...' she began, but he was already hurrying towards the lift. He waited until the porters had wheeled out the trolley then disappeared.

Emma smiled to herself as she went to meet the new patient. It was all systems go but it was good to be part of the team and feel needed. Was that why she was enjoying helping Daniel make this Christmas special for Amy?

It was a simple enough explanation yet Emma knew in her heart that the answer was far more complex than that. She frowned as she tried to work it out but it was rather like one of those maths problems—if you added A to B then added C, what did you get?

She tried substituting names for the letters to see if that made it any clearer.

Daniel plus Amy plus herself equalled...what?

A happy family?

Of course not! No wonder maths had been her worst subject at school if that was the kind of answer she came up with!

CHAPTER SEVEN

IT WAS almost two a.m. before the all-clear was given. It had been a hectic night and Emma was glad that it was over. There had been fourteen casualties brought into the hospital but, amazingly, only two were in a critical condition. All in all, it could have been an awful lot worse, she reflected as she went to collect a tired-looking Amy.

'Can we go home now, Emma?' the little girl asked as soon as she saw her.

'We can, indeed. We have to meet Uncle Daniel downstairs. He'll be waiting in the foyer for us so let's go and get our coats.'

Emma led Amy to the staffroom. She smiled as she opened the door and saw Linda leaning against the lockers with her eyes closed. 'No sleeping on the job, Nurse Wood!'

'I'm bushed.' Linda didn't bother opening her eyes. 'I've been on autopilot for the past hour. To think I'd planned to spend the evening in front of the telly, watching that new hospital drama.'

'But instead you found yourself playing a starring role in our very own version,' Emma teased. 'Who says that real life doesn't mirror fiction, or is it vice versa?'

'I dunno. I'm too tired to care anyway.' Linda opened one eye and stared blearily at her. 'I've no idea why you're so perky at this time of the night.'

'Oh, I could hazard a guess.' Jane had arrived back from the A and E unit where she'd been helping to register the casualties as they'd been brought in. She shot a pointed look at Amy and grinned. 'They say that love overcomes all obstacles so maybe that includes bad backs and aching feet!'

Emma blushed furiously, although she didn't say anything. She quickly took Amy's coat from her locker and helped the child to zip it up.

'Anyway, your Daniel was a huge hit in A and E, Emma.' Jane was in the process of shedding her uniform and her voice was muffled as she dragged the top over her head. 'I think he's added several more members to his fan club tonight.'

'He isn't *my* Daniel,' Emma corrected her, conscious that Amy was listening to what was being said. 'I told you that I'm just helping him out.'

'Hmm, well, there's helping and then again there's *helping,* isn't there?' Jane teased, pulling on her sweater.

Emma rolled her eyes. 'I give up! Think what you like. I know what the truth is!'

She headed for the door then paused when she saw Mike Humphreys standing there. He gave her an odd look but carried on along the corridor without saying anything. Emma sighed as she realised that Mike still appeared to be nursing a grudge. She didn't want to fall out with him but there was no way that she was going to apologise when she didn't believe she'd been at fault.

'Hold on! I'm coming with you.'

Linda caught up with them and they went down in the lift together. There were a lot of staff milling about in the foyer. Emma looked round but she couldn't see any sign of Daniel.

'Daniel said to tell you that he's been held up.' Ruby Jones, one of the senior staff nurses on A and E, tapped Emma on the shoulder. 'He said that he'd be grateful if you'd take Amy home with you and he'll collect her as soon as he can.'

'Oh, right. Thanks, Ruby.' Emma sighed as the other

woman hurried away. 'I suppose I'd better see if I can find a taxi.'

'Don't be daft. I'll drop you off on my way,' Linda offered immediately.

'Would you? Oh, thanks, Linda. I'd appreciate it.' Emma turned to Amy with a smile. 'It looks as though you'll be staying at my flat until Uncle Daniel can leave the hospital. Is that OK?'

Amy nodded solemnly. 'Does that mean I can sleep in your bed, Emma?'

'You'll have to, seeing as I only have one bed. Still, it's a big bed so there'll be plenty of room for us both.'

Emma took hold of the child's hand as they left the building. The wind had died down now that the storm had passed. It was still raining, however, so she quickened her pace as they hurried to where Linda had parked her car.

'Where will Uncle Daniel sleep? Is your bed big enough for him as well?' Amy asked in all innocence.

'Out of the mouths of babes, eh, Emma?' Linda teased as she unlocked the car doors.

Emma pretended that she hadn't heard the remark as she helped Amy into the car. 'Don't worry about that now, Amy,' she said firmly. 'Let's just concentrate on getting home.'

Thankfully, Amy let the subject drop. Linda didn't mention it again either, although Emma knew that it wouldn't have been forgotten. She sighed as she fastened her seat belt. When would people accept that she was only helping Daniel as any friend would have done?

Maybe when *she* believed it herself, a small voice whispered silkily.

Emma's lips compressed. She didn't intend even to think about that!

It didn't take long to get Amy ready for bed. The child was almost asleep on her feet. Emma found one of her T-shirts for the little girl to wear in the absence of any proper night-wear. She tucked Amy up in one side of the big double bed then quickly undressed and slid beneath the quilt. She, too, fell asleep almost as soon as her head touched the pillow and didn't stir until the sound of the doorbell ringing woke her just before nine.

Emma struggled out of bed and dragged on a dressing-gown. Amy was still fast asleep so she took care not to wake her. She ran down the stairs and opened the front door to find Daniel on the step. He looked grey with fatigue, his shoulders slumping tiredly as he propped himself against the wall.

'Hi. Sorry it took so long to get here. I ended up in Theatre, dealing with an abruption of the placenta,' he explained. 'Fortunately, the baby was viable so we were able to do a Caesarean, but the mother was very shocked.'

'Will she be all right?' Emma asked worriedly. When the placenta suddenly separated from its bed it could cause a lot of problems. The main risk was to the baby because of the interruption to the blood supply it received via the placenta. Shock and blood loss were the most dangerous side effects for the mother and always required urgent hospital treatment.

'I think so, but it was touch and go at one stage which is why it took so long. Anyway, I decided that I might as well collect Amy on my way home rather than come back for her later.'

'She's still asleep, I'm afraid. Look, why don't you come in and have a cup of coffee?' Emma offered immediately.

Daniel hesitated. 'I don't want to disturb you, although it's probably a bit late to worry about that. Were you asleep as well when I rang the bell, Emma?'

He sighed when she nodded. 'Sorry! I feel really guilty about waking you up now. Look, you go on back to bed. You can phone me whenever you're ready and I'll come back for Amy.'

He started to leave but Emma stopped him. 'Don't be silly. I'm up now so there's no point in me going back to bed. Come in and have that coffee. You look as though you need it, quite frankly.'

'Well, if you're sure…?' Daniel shrugged. 'OK. You've talked me into it. Actually, a cup of coffee would be great. I've just about reached the point where my eyes are open but the rest of me has gone to sleep!'

'Then you certainly shouldn't be driving in that state!' Emma said firmly. 'Or it will be you having an accident if you're not careful.'

Daniel laughed. 'Yes, Staff!'

Emma laughed with him then led the way upstairs to her flat. 'Go into the sitting room and make yourself comfortable while I make the coffee. Could you manage some toast to go with it?'

'Please.' Daniel sighed ruefully. 'It seems an age since we had those fish and chips, doesn't it? I'm starving.'

He ambled into the sitting room, leaving Emma to hurry to the kitchen to make coffee and toast. She loaded everything onto a tray then took it through to the sitting room, pausing when she discovered that Daniel was sprawled out on her sofa, fast asleep.

Emma quietly put the tray on the coffee-table and went to fetch a blanket to cover him with. He murmured as she tucked it around him but he didn't wake up. Emma smiled as she studied his sleeping face. He was obviously worn out after the hectic night and would probably sleep for hours if he got the chance.

She poured herself a cup of the coffee then sat down while she drank it, watching Daniel while he slept. It felt right to have him here in her flat just as it felt right to know that Amy was asleep in her bed. Funny how important Daniel and his niece had become to her in such a short time. It made her realise how hard it was going to be once Christmas was over. She'd promised Daniel that she would help him give Amy a very special Christmas, but it was a gift which came with strings attached. It wasn't going to be easy to cut them and walk away afterwards.

Amy awoke a short time later. Emma went to the bedroom as soon as she heard the little girl moving around.

'Good morning, Amy. You had a nice long sleep, didn't you? Are you hungry?'

Amy nodded sleepily. 'Can I have my breakfast here with you, Emma, before Uncle Daniel comes?'

'Uncle Daniel is already here, darling. He arrived a few minutes ago but he was so tired that he's fallen asleep on the sofa.' Emma smiled as Amy giggled. 'Shall we try to be very quiet so that we don't wake him up?'

The child thought it was a marvellous game, tiptoeing around the flat. Emma took her into the kitchen and gave her a bowl of cornflakes and some orange juice then sent her to get washed and dressed. Daniel was still fast asleep when Emma checked on him so she decided there was no point in waking him up. She wrote him a brief note to let him know that she was taking Amy to the shops then they set off.

They spent a very pleasant couple of hours, pottering around the shops. With there being only a week or so to go before Christmas, most of the town's traders had decided to open that Sunday. Emma bought a few small gifts for her friends at work then helped Amy choose a present for Daniel. It wasn't easy, finding something the child thought would be just right for him, but in the end Amy decided on a bright blue tie patterned all over with bells and holly. Emma couldn't help smiling as she pictured Daniel wearing it with one his elegant suits!

It was almost noon when they arrived back at the flat. Emma let them in then crept into the sitting room, expecting to find Daniel still asleep. However, the only sign of him was the neatly folded blanket on the sofa, and she frowned. Had he decided to go home when he'd discovered that she and Amy had gone out?

'Hi, there. Have you two had a good time, then?'

Emma spun round as Daniel suddenly appeared. She felt her eyes widen as she took in what he was wearing, which was very little! He must have just got out of the shower, and one of her pink towels wrapped around his hips was all he had on.

Emma felt her mouth go dry as she was presented with the sight of his muscular body. In a fast sweep her eyes took note of the tanned skin drawn tautly over those well-honed muscles, the thick, dark curls which covered his broad chest. Droplets of water sparkled in his hair. As Emma watched, a bead of water dropped onto his shoulder and began to trickle down his chest. Her eyes seemed to be mesmerised as she followed its progress…

She turned away, feeling shaken by the way she was behaving. She had seen other men naked before—it would be amazing if she hadn't, considering the job she did! However, there was no way that she could compare how she'd felt on those occasions with how she felt at that moment, her body aching in a way she barely understood.

'Emma? Are you OK?' Daniel asked. He paused and she heard the faint uncertainty in his voice when he continued, 'You didn't mind me taking a shower, did you?'

'Of course not! Don't be silly.' Her tone was a shade too bright and she saw his eyes darken with puzzlement. She hurried on, wanting to distract him before he worked out why she was behaving so strangely. It was bad enough knowing how Daniel affected her, without him realising it as well!

'I was just a bit surprised when you appeared like that. When I saw that you weren't in the sitting room I assumed that you'd gone home.'

'I've only just woken up,' he explained quietly. 'I read your note so I thought I'd take a shower while you and

Amy were out. Then I'd be ready to take her home when you got back.'

He turned to his niece and Emma had the funniest feeling that it was just an excuse to avoid looking at her. Why? What was it that Daniel didn't want her to see?

'So, what have you bought, then? Aren't you going to show me?'

She pushed the thought to the back of her mind as Amy shook her head. 'I can't tell you, Uncle Daniel, 'cos it's a secret!'

'Oh, is it, indeed? A secret, eh? I wonder what *sort* of a secret,' he teased the little girl.

'It's a present for you but you have to wait till Christmas Day to see what it is!' Amy couldn't quite manage to keep it to herself and Emma laughed.

'Don't tell him anything else, Amy! It won't be so much fun if you spoil the surprise.'

'Whose side are you on, you wicked woman?' Daniel's tone was dry as he turned to her. 'I thought you were a nice kind person but here you are encouraging this little horror to torment the life out of me. I don't know if I can last till Christmas Day without knowing what my present is!'

'Tough!' Emma declared unsympathetically. 'You'll just have to learn to be patient, won't you? Anyway, it's only just over a week until Christmas Day. I'm sure you can wait that long!'

'I suppose I shall have to, seeing as you two females have ganged up on me.' Daniel tried to look suitably pathetic but failed miserably. He gave a heavy sigh when Amy giggled. 'I can see that I'm not going to persuade you two to take pity on me so I may as well get dressed. But it's tit for tat, don't forget. If you won't show me my present then I won't show you yours!'

Emma laughed as he stalked away. 'Isn't he naughty, trying to get you to show him his present, Amy? I tell you what, why don't you wrap it up before he comes back? That way he won't get chance to peek at it.'

She found the child some colourful Christmas paper and helped her to wrap the tie. Amy insisted on using several sheets of paper and yards of sticky tape. Emma chuckled as she looked at the lumpy package. 'Well, I don't think there's much danger of Daniel managing to undo that in a hurry.'

'What are you up to now?' Daniel came back into the room, fully dressed now. He laughed as Amy ran to show him the present. 'Can I just have a little squeeze?' he wheedled. 'Maybe I can work out what it is…'

'No! That's naughty, Uncle Daniel.' Amy whipped the present out of his reach and turned appealingly to Emma. 'Tell him he's not to do that, Emma.'

'You most certainly mustn't. Father Christmas takes a very dim view of people who try to peek at their presents before Christmas Day,' she warned him solemnly, trying not to laugh.

'I shall bear it in mind. I don't want to wake up on Christmas morning and find my stocking is empty. All right, I promise that I'll behave from now on,' he replied with suitable solemnity, although his eyes were sparkling with laughter. 'Anyway, it's time that Amy and I were on our way. We've taken up enough of your time one way and another, Emma. Thanks for having Amy to stay last night and for looking after her while I was in A and E. I really appreciate it.'

'It was my pleasure,' she told him sincerely. She gave the child a hug when Amy came running to her. 'You must come and stay here again some time. Would you like that?'

'Oh, yes!' Amy turned to Daniel. 'Emma has a really big bed, Uncle Daniel, so you could stay, too,' she explained guilelessly.

'Mmm, I think it's time we left,' Daniel declared. There seemed to be more amusement in his voice than anything else, Emma noticed. There certainly wasn't any indication that he found the idea of spending the night in her bed tempting!

Emma didn't know why she should feel disappointed. However, she did her best to hide her feelings as she saw him and Amy out. Daniel paused on the step. 'Thanks again, Emma. I really do appreciate everything you've done.'

He kissed her lightly on the cheek then hurried to his car. Amy waved as they drove away and Emma waved back. She closed the door as the car disappeared from sight and went back upstairs. She had a lot to do that day—washing, ironing, cleaning—all the hundred and one jobs which accumulated while she was out at work. However, her mind was only partly on what she was doing as she started loading the washing machine. Her thoughts were mainly of Daniel and what had happened in the past week.

She sighed as she added detergent to the machine. How had he become such a major part of her life in such a short time?

Most of the extra patients had been moved from the ward by the time Emma arrived for work on Monday morning. However, Maria Carstairs, the patient who'd been threatening to miscarry, was still there.

Fortunately, Daniel's prompt treatment appeared to have worked and there was a good chance that Maria's baby would go to term. She was staying in the ward for a few more days as a precaution, but everyone was cautiously optimistic that the danger had been averted. Emma went to speak to her in the middle of the morning and found Maria looking a lot better than when she'd been admitted on the Saturday night.

'No need to ask how you are,' she said cheerfully, automatically checking Maria's chart. 'You look a lot better than the last time I saw you.'

Maria frowned. 'I'm sorry, I don't seem to remember you. It was all such a nightmare, you understand. I was so scared that I was going to lose the baby.'

'It must have been awful for you,' Emma sympathised. 'It's no wonder you don't remember everyone's faces. I was here when Dr Hutton brought you up from A and E.'

'I remember Dr Hutton. How could I forget him?' Maria's face broke into a warm smile. 'He was so kind to me. Rob, that's my husband, well, Rob said that if it hadn't been for Dr Hutton we would have lost the baby. Is that right?'

'Oh, I think it's fair to say that,' Emma said lightly, feeling a little rush of pride at the thought of the role Daniel had played in helping to save Maria's baby. 'He's a wonderful doctor and all the patients like him.'

'Obviously, you think very highly of him, Nurse,' Maria observed, and Emma blushed. She hadn't realised how revealing her comments had been.

'We all do,' she explained carefully, and excused herself as she saw that Sister Carter was trying to attract her attention to warn her that the ward round was about to begin.

She hurried to fetch the patients' notes because she knew how Max Dennison hated to be kept waiting, but when she came back with the trolley it was to find that Daniel was taking the round that day. He had Mike with him, as well as Tina Majors, the obs and gynae junior registrar. Sister Carter took her aside and quietly explained that Mr Dennison was off sick that day so Daniel was standing in for him.

Emma left them to carry on because there was always a lot to do throughout the day. However, she couldn't help wondering how it would affect Daniel's schedule if he had to step in for his chief for a prolonged period. That it might have repercussions on the amount of time he could spend with Amy was another worrying thought.

She made up her mind to have a word with him and

offer to help in any way she could. Amy would be breaking up from school in the next few days so that could cause a problem. And there was all the shopping still to be done— the food and all the other things which needed to be bought. With Christmas now less than a week away there was an awful lot to get ready.

Emma had no chance to speak to Daniel after the ward round because Sister Carter was keen to discuss the adjustments that had been made to various patients' treatment. Shirley Rogers's temperature was still causing some concern and Daniel had increased the level of antibiotics she was receiving. It meant that Shirley would be staying with them a bit longer and the poor woman was very disappointed. Emma found her close to tears when she stopped by her bed after Sister Carter had disappeared into the office with Daniel and his entourage.

'Why did I have to get this stupid infection?' Shirley demanded, blowing her nose on a very damp tissue. 'I thought I would have been discharged today and now it looks as though I might still be here on Christmas Day! I don't know what my Ron and the boys are going to do without me there to cook the dinner for them.'

'There's still time for you to be allowed to go home, Shirley, although I have to say that it would be very silly of you to go rushing around,' Emma warned. 'Surely your husband and sons can manage for once?'

'Oh, I don't know about that…' Shirley shook her head. 'I can't see any of them setting to and stuffing a turkey, can you, love?'

Emma laughed at that. She'd met Shirley's husband and sons and could understand her concerns. All four of the Rogers men were very down to earth but she doubted that they'd seen any need to learn how to cook when they had Shirley to do it for them.

'No, I can't, I'm afraid. It's your fault for spoiling them, Shirley.'

'I can't help it. I think I must just be made that way. I enjoy looking after them, although I know that isn't the politically correct thing to say.' Shirley laughed. 'I suppose I must seem very old-fashioned to a young woman like you.'

Emma shook her head. Her tone was unconsciously wistful as she thought about how much she was enjoying looking after Amy and, in a way, Daniel. 'No, I don't think that at all. I imagine it's very satisfying to take care of the people you love. But don't forget that it works two ways. Maybe Ron and the boys would enjoy having the chance to look after you for once.'

Shirley nodded thoughtfully. 'You could be right at that. Thanks, love. You've cheered me up a bit.'

'My pleasure,' Emma declared with a grin, before she went to prepare a patient who would be going to Theatre shortly. All the time she was running through the familiar routine, her mind kept playing with the thought of how hard it was going to be after Christmas when there was only herself to look after. Being part of a family, even if it was only for a short time, was something to treasure.

In the end it was Daniel who sought Emma out. She'd not had time to speak to him because he'd been due in Theatre after leaving the ward. She was on her way to the canteen for lunch when he caught up with her by the lift.

'Can you spare a minute, Emma?' he asked, nodding pleasantly to Linda and Eileen.

'Of course.' Emma turned to her friends, trying to ignore the knowing looks they were giving her. 'I'll catch you up in a minute.'

'Don't rush. We'll save you a seat.' Linda treated her to a wicked smile and Emma groaned as she realised that she would be in line for the third degree when she did join them! However, there was no point worrying about it right then so she put it out of her mind and followed Daniel into the television lounge, which was empty at that moment. He looked so harassed, anyway, that her main concern was what might be wrong.

'Problems?' she asked, perching on the arm of a chair.

'How did you guess?' He sighed as he sank heavily onto the chair opposite. 'You know that Max is off sick. Well, evidently, he's been having chest pains for several weeks but has ignored them. However, it got so bad last night that his wife had to call his GP.

'Anyway, the outcome of it all is that Max is suffering from angina and he's been told that he has to take time off work while they sort out his treatment.'

'Really? He always seems so fit. He certainly rushes around like a man half his age,' Emma exclaimed.

'I know, although I've noticed on a couple of occasions that he appeared to be in some sort of discomfort. He passed it off when I asked him if he was all right, said that it was indigestion. Obviously, it was more serious than that,' Daniel explained dryly.

Emma sighed. 'Sounds about right. Medical professionals are the world's worst at admitting that there might be anything wrong with them!'

Daniel laughed. 'Amen to that! But it does mean that with Max off my workload is going to virtually double, and that's going to create no end of problems at the moment.'

'You know that I'll do anything I can to help,' Emma offered immediately.

'Thanks. I was hoping you'd say that, even though I feel guilty for putting on you like this.' Daniel's smile was warm and Emma shrugged, not wanting him to guess how it affected her. Just a smile and her heart was singing arias. Crazy!

'Don't be silly. Just tell me how I can help you.'

'Well, first off is the shopping. I had been planning on taking a couple of days off this week to get everything done, but that's out of the question now. Is there any chance I can leave it to you, Emma?'

He ran his hand through his hair and sighed. 'It's not only the food that needs to be bought but Amy's presents as well. I just haven't had chance to get round to doing it, you see.'

'I'll be happy to get anything you need. Luckily I'm off from the twenty-third right through till after Boxing Day so I'll have plenty of time to do it.'

'Are you sure? I don't want you spending all your free time on this. You must have other things planned, apart from Amy's Christmas!'

Daniel laughed ruefully and Emma smiled. 'Nothing that can't wait, believe me. No, I'm happy to do it, Daniel. Honestly, I am.'

He took a deep breath and his eyes shone with something she found impossible to understand. 'Thank you, Emma. I just don't know what I would have done if you hadn't offered to help me.'

'You'd have managed somehow,' she said, smiling at him. 'Anyway, I'm looking forward to it. I want it to be a very special Christmas, too!'

'Oh, it will be. I don't have any doubts about that.' Daniel glanced round as the door opened. His smiled faded when he saw Mike Humphreys. 'Did you want me?' he asked coolly.

'Max is on the phone. He needs to speak to you urgently,' Mike told him flatly.

Daniel got up at once. 'I'd better see what he wants. He won't do himself any good if he keeps worrying about what's going on here.' He glanced at Emma. 'I'll catch you later, Emma. OK?'

He hurried away as Emma got up and went to the door. Mike was still standing there and he looked quizzically at her. 'You two seem to be getting very pally of late. Linda said that you're helping Hutton with his niece or something.'

Emma quelled the urge to tell him to mind his own business. Maybe this was the opportunity she'd been looking for to smooth over their differences. 'That's right. Daniel asked me if I'd help him get everything ready for Christmas.'

'It's a shame, isn't it? I feel sorry for the poor kid.' Mike hurried on when she looked at him. 'It must be hard on her, losing her mother at such a young age, I mean.'

Emma smiled more warmly at him. Maybe Mike wasn't quite as insensitive as she'd thought him to be. He was obviously concerned about Amy and that had to be a point in his favour. 'It is a shame. Amy is only six and it must have been a huge wrench for her, losing her mother. Still, Daniel's making a marvellous job of looking after her.'

'I'm sure he is.' Mike smiled easily when she shot him a sharp look. She couldn't help wondering if there had been a trace of sarcasm in his voice. However, she couldn't see any sign of it and immediately felt guilty that she should keep misjudging him all the time.

'Look, Em, you and I seem to have got our signals crossed somehow or other. I hate to think that we can't be friends so can we forget what happened the other day?'

'If that's what you want, of course we can, Mike,' she agreed immediately, feeling worse than ever when she saw how anxious he looked. Obviously, her friendship meant a lot to him.

'Oh, that's great!' He gave her a wide smile. 'It's a weight off my mind, I can tell you. So, to prove that we're friends again, will you come to the staff dance with me after all?'

'Oh, well, I'm not sure—' she began, but Mike didn't let her finish.

'Come on, say you will! I was so looking forward to having you as my partner and I won't feel that we've cleared the air unless you agree,' he added persuasively.

Emma sighed because she wasn't sure what to do. She didn't want to fall out with Mike again by refusing, but she wasn't sure if she had the time to go when there was so much to do.

'Maybe you've had a better offer.' Mike sounded disappointed. 'I don't blame you if you'd prefer to go to the dance with Daniel Hutton.'

'That isn't it at all,' she said quickly, wanting to stem any rumours before they had chance to circulate. 'I'm helping Daniel with his Christmas arrangements, but we certainly aren't going *out* together.'

'Then say you'll come to the dance. I don't expect you to stay all night if you have things to do, but it would mean a lot to me, Em.'

Emma's tender heart went out to Mike as he pleaded with her. What harm would there be in spending a couple of hours at the dance? She would have plenty of time to help Daniel. All he wanted her for was to help him make Amy's Christmas perfect. It wasn't as though he wanted her company for any other reason.

The thought was so deflating that it spurred Emma into making up her mind. It was about time she started trying to build up her social life. Once Christmas was over with there would be a big gap in her life. She would have to find a way to fill it one way or another.

'All right, then, I'll come. But I might not be able to stay all night.'

'Oh, don't worry about that. So long as you come, that's all I'm interested in.'

Emma frowned as Mike quickly said goodbye and hurried away. Was it her imagination again or had there been something behind that last statement?

She sighed as it struck her that she was in danger of misjudging the young house officer once again. Or was it that she was in danger of judging him against Daniel?

Could any man bear such a comparison and come out on top? she wondered as she went for her lunch. Unlikely. Highly unlikely. Daniel Hutton was head and shoulders above any other man she knew. It would be very hard to find anyone to measure up to him.

Her mouth curved into a sad little smile. The thought of spending her life looking for someone to match up to Daniel wasn't an appealing prospect at all.

CHAPTER EIGHT

DANIEL was waiting for Emma when she left the hospital that evening. He drew her aside out of the way of the flow of people making their way in and out of the building.

'I won't keep you long,' he told her quickly. 'I just thought it might be useful if I gave you this.'

He handed her a key. 'It's a key to my house. It seems pointless, you having to haul bags of shopping home to your flat and then me having to collect them later, doesn't it? You may as well take them straight to the house.'

'It would be a lot easier, if you don't mind,' Emma agreed.

'Of course I don't mind! You just go in whenever you need to, Emma. You don't need to check with me beforehand either.'

'Right, I'll do that.' Emma sighed. 'I could do with a list of the things you want me to buy, though, Daniel. I don't mean the food and stuff like that, but the presents you want me to get for Amy.'

'I've already thought of that. Here you are.' He handed her a list, grinning when she frowned. 'Sorry about the writing. I wrote it in a bit of a hurry.'

'I can tell. What does this say? Chocolate monkey?' Emma pointed to a line of the scrawled black script and Daniel laughed out loud.

'Chocolate *money!* You know, those foil-wrapped chocolate coins you get in a little net bag. Amy loves them and I remember that Claire always used to make a point of buying her some each Christmas.' Daniel shook his head. 'If there's a *monkey* around here, it's you, Emma Graham.

You're a real cheeky monkey for being so rude about my handwriting.'

'Rude? I was being honest.' Emma laughed up at him. 'A spider with its legs dipped in ink could have made a better job of writing this! Typical doctor's handwriting, though. I have no idea how you lot ever pass any exams when nobody can read your writing.'

'Oh, the rot only sets in *after* you've passed all your exams. It's pressure of work, you see—something you nurses know very little about…' He held up his hand when she opened her mouth. 'Just teasing. Honest!'

'I should hope so, too,' Emma declared loftily, although she could feel a smile playing around her lips. It was such fun to swop banter with Daniel like this. It was hard to remember that only a week ago their conversation had been nothing more remarkable than a discussion about a patient's progress! They had come a long way in a very short time, it seemed. But, then, necessity had been the deciding factor for the change in their relationship. Daniel had needed her help and that was why his attitude towards her had changed so dramatically.

It was a sobering thought because it brought it home to her how ephemeral their present relationship was—it would probably revert to normal once Christmas was over. Emma suddenly knew that she was going to miss these engaging exchanges they had but, then, she was going to miss a lot of other things as well. Being part of Daniel's life had given an added meaning to her own life. It wasn't going to be easy to go back to how things had been before all this had happened.

She realised that Daniel had said something while she'd been daydreaming. 'Sorry? I didn't catch that.'

'I was just checking that you would be in this evening around six-thirty,' he explained. 'I've arranged for one of the local garages to bring a car round to your flat and thought that would be the most convenient time for them to call.'

'A car?' Emma repeated, not sure that she'd heard him correctly.

'That's right. I don't want you trying to lug all this shopping about on the bus, Emma. It's far too heavy for you. I've arranged for you to have a hire car for the next week which should help.'

'That's really kind of you, Daniel. Are you sure, though? I never expected anything like this.' She couldn't hide her surprise and she saw his eyes darken. He half reached towards her then stopped and looked around as though he'd suddenly remembered that they were standing in full view of anyone going in or out of the hospital. And when he spoke his voice held a note which made Emma's heart catch as though it had suddenly forgotten how to beat.

'I know that you didn't expect it, Emma. I doubt if you even thought about the inconvenience it would cause you, having to go rushing about with heavy shopping bags. Putting other people first seems to come naturally to you. It's about time that someone put you first for a change.'

He gave her the most gentle smile that she'd seen on anyone's face. Her heart gave a small hiccup then it was off and running, sending the blood shooting through her veins and making her feel dizzy. Emma managed to smile back but it was an effort when what she really wanted to do at that moment was cry her eyes out. To know that Daniel cared about her this much seemed to have touched a raw spot inside.

How many times had she longed to have someone to care about her, to look after her, to love her? How many times had she longed to have someone to care for, to look after, to love? Could that someone she'd been looking for all her life be Daniel?

Someone jostled her arm and she took a shaky breath. Her head was spinning and her mind was too crowded to think of pleasantries, yet anything else would have been unthinkable. Daniel was just trying to be kind. It would be foolish to let herself read more into his actions than might have been intended.

'I…I appreciate your thoughtfulness,' she told him flatly, because she was desperate to keep any trace of emotion out of her voice. 'It will be a great help, having a car to use. I'll be able to go into Bournemouth and get some of the shopping there. There's a much better selection in the shops there than there is here in Clearsea.'

'Good. So long as it makes life easier for you.' Daniel's tone was brisk once more as he dug into his pocket and pulled out an envelope. 'I don't want you having to pay for the shopping yourself so take this, Emma. And promise me that you'll tell me if you need more money.'

Her eyes stung as she slid the envelope into her pocket without even glancing at it. It hurt to have their relationship reduced to a simple business arrangement, though she knew that it wasn't what he'd intended to do. Daniel was just trying to make life as easy as possible for her, and yet…

'I'll let you have a receipt for whatever I buy,' she told him, refusing to let herself go any further. She shook her head when it looked as though he was going to object. 'I'd prefer it, if you don't mind.'

'Of course, it's up to you.' Daniel's tone was emotionless. Nevertheless, Emma shot him a look from under her lashes, wondering why she had a feeling that he was annoyed. However, there was no trace of anything on his face to reinforce that idea so she dismissed it.

Stick to the facts, Emma! she told herself firmly. The fact is, you're helping Daniel out of a difficult situation. He's grateful to you so naturally he wants to be as helpful as possible, which is why he's arranged for the car and given you the money. Easy when you think about it, isn't it? So stop looking for problems!

'I won't detain you any longer. I'd offer you a lift only

I have to finish some paperwork that Max hadn't got round to doing.' Daniel sighed as he glanced at his watch. 'Hopefully, I should have it done by six so I won't need to leave Amy with the childminder too much longer.'

It was on the tip of Emma's tongue to offer to fetch the little girl but she decided against it. She didn't want Daniel thinking that she was overstepping the line and trying to take on too big a role in his life.

She said goodbye and hurried away to catch her bus. She was just in time because it arrived as soon as she got to the stop. Emma climbed aboard and paid her fare then sat staring out of the window as it trundled through the town.

The streets were ablaze with Christmas lights and it seemed that every house she passed had a tree in its window. With six days to go, the excitement was mounting. Emma realised that she felt excited about it herself, although she'd never really enjoyed Christmas before. This year was different, of course, because she wouldn't be on her own and would have someone to share it with. However, there was a bitter-sweetness to the thought.

One glorious and very special day then it would be over. Daniel and Amy wouldn't need her after that.

Emma arrived at work the following day to find the ward in a state of chaos. Paula Walters had discovered that her engagement ring was missing and so far nobody had been able to find out what had become of it.

'The silly woman. Fancy leaving an expensive ring like that lying around.'

Sister Carter's tone was scathing but Emma knew that it was because she was worried that the finger of suspicion might point to one of the staff. It was rare for anything to go missing but whenever it had happened in the past it had left a nasty taste in everyone's mouth. It wasn't pleasant to wonder if someone you'd been working with might be a thief.

'I did offer to put the ring in the office safe,' Emma said sadly. She saw Sister Carter's surprise and hurried to explain, wondering why she felt guilty all of a sudden. That was another horrible side effect when something like this happened—it tended to make *everyone* feel on edge.

'Paula asked me to find her fiancé's phone number in her diary and happened to mention in passing that her engagement ring was in the pocket of her bag. I offered to put it in the safe but she said that she preferred to keep it with her.'

'I see. I wonder if anyone else heard what she said? Can you remember, Emma?' Sister Carter sighed. 'The puzzling thing about this is that only the ring is missing. Paula's bag was still in her locker and she swears that she hasn't taken the ring out of it since she's been here.

'I couldn't understand how anyone knew it was there but perhaps this explains it. Maybe someone overheard your conversation? Or maybe Paula told someone else as well?'

Emma frowned. 'I honestly don't remember anyone else being around at the time. Paula is in the end bed next to the folding doors so there may have been someone visiting a patient in the obstetric unit.'

'Possible. Although surely we would have noticed a stranger poking around in Paula's locker?' Sister Carter shook her head in exasperation. 'I don't know what the answer is. We'll have to leave it to the police to see if they can find out what's happened to it. It could turn out that the wretched ring is in Paula's house and she simply *thought* that she'd brought it with her.'

'Let's hope so,' Emma replied quietly, because she couldn't help thinking what an awkward position it put her in if she was the only one who had known about the ring being in Paula's bag.

There was little time to dwell on the matter, however, as the day got off to yet another busy start. The ectopic pregnancy patient Daniel had dealt with a few days earlier was moved down to the ward from the IC unit. The woman's name was Fleur Simmonds, a pretty redhead in her early twenties. Emma got her settled in after her transfer to the ward.

'It's nice to be out of that place,' Fleur declared as Emma finished straightening the bedclothes. 'It's really scary when you wake up and find yourself surrounded by all that equipment.'

'It must be. But the IC unit is the best place to be when a patient is very ill, like you were, Fleur. You received individual nursing care, which is impossible to give on the average ward.'

'Oh, I know that. And I'm really grateful for it, too,' Fleur said quickly. 'I know that it was touch and go at one point and that if I hadn't had such a wonderful doctor and nurses to look after me I might not have made it.'

She shuddered expressively. 'I never guessed that there was anything wrong with me until it happened. Surely I should have realised something wasn't quite right?'

'Sometimes it happens that way with an ectopic pregnancy,' Emma assured her. 'There are no indications at all until a woman suffers severe abdominal pain and bleeding. All the symptoms of being pregnant are just the same as if the pregnancy were normal so there's no reason to suspect anything is wrong. That's why it can be so dangerous.'

'Dr Hutton explained that he'd had to remove one of my Fallopian tubes because it was badly damaged.' Fleur looked sad.

Emma knew what she was thinking and hurried to re-assure her, even though she knew that Daniel would have explained what it could mean. However, sometimes a woman needed to be told more than once that it wasn't all doom and gloom.

'That's right—but it doesn't mean that you won't be able to conceive again, Fleur. Naturally, it does slightly reduce the chances of you getting pregnant, but most women who've had ectopic pregnancies do go on to have another baby.'

'That's what Dr Hutton told me. I shall just have to look on the bright side, won't I?' Fleur said positively.

'You will,' Emma agreed with a smile. 'I bet it won't be long before you're booking into St Luke's again, only it will be into the maternity unit next time!'

Fleur laughed at that. Emma left her to rest because she knew that Fleur must still be feeling weak after what had happened to her. Shirley Rogers was looking a lot better that morning because her temperature had come down. When Emma stopped by her bed she was full of what might have happened to the missing engagement ring.

'I can't understand it going missing like that, can you, love? I mean, there's nobody here who'd take it!' Shirley declared forcibly.

'I agree. I just hope it turns up soon, though.' Emma grimaced. 'It's not nice, feeling that you're under suspicion.'

'I wonder if Paula imagined that she had it in her bag,' Shirley said *sotto voce*. 'I've done things like that myself more than once, I can tell you—imagined that I've done something or other and I haven't. I mean, Paula was in a right state when she was brought in so it would be easy to get a bit confused, wouldn't it?'

'It would. Fingers crossed that the ring turns up at her home, safely tucked in a drawer!' Emma declared. 'Anyway, how are you feeling this morning?'

'Fine. I've got my fingers *and* my toes crossed that I'll be allowed to go home soon, although how I'm going to get all my shopping done I have no idea!'

'I would write out a list and send one of your sons to do it, if I were you. Tell them that Christmas is cancelled if they don't play Santa's little helpers!'

Shirley laughed then clutched her stitches. 'Santa's little

helpers, indeed. The three of them are over six feet tall and built like rugby players!'

Emma left Shirley still chuckling at the idea. Eileen Pierce was off sick that day so they were busier than ever with one member of staff short. She was ready for a break by the time lunchtime came around.

Linda went with her to the canteen and they queued up for their lunch. Emma loaded a portion of cottage pie onto her tray then added a bottle of fizzy mineral water. She looked round for a place to sit, while Linda debated the merits of the cottage pie or the chilli, and couldn't help noticing that people seemed to be looking at her.

'Do you ever have the feeling that you've got a smut on your nose or something?' she murmured to Linda as they made their way to an empty table. 'Why is everyone staring like that?'

'Probably stunned by your beauty, Emma!' Linda laughed as she plonked her tray on the table. 'They say that a woman in love has a certain *glow* about her.'

Emma rolled her eyes. 'I won't even dignify that with an answer!' She unloaded her tray then shot a wary look over her shoulder, but nobody seemed to be looking their way.

'Must be getting paranoid,' she muttered, picking up her fork and digging into the lukewarm meal.

'Maybe. Or maybe everyone is speculating about you and Daniel. Come on, Em, you don't honestly expect folk to believe that there's nothing going on between you two.'

'There isn't. I'm just helping him out, that's all.' Emma forked up another mouthful of the cottage pie and chewed it slowly, though it tasted just a degree better than atrocious.

'Then I despair! What are you, a woman or a mouse? How can you let a gorgeous hunk like Daniel Hutton slip through your fingers without trying to do something about it?' Linda glared her displeasure. 'You're a disgrace to womankind, Emma Graham!'

Emma laughed. 'And you're a complete idiot. Anyway, it takes two to tango, as the saying goes. I…I don't get the impression that Daniel has any ideas about me *that* way.'

'But you'd like him to, wouldn't you?' Linda leaned across the table. 'I can tell I'm right, Emma. You do fancy him, don't you?'

Emma shrugged. 'Maybe, but I don't think Daniel is in the market for a relationship and if he was, why would he choose me?'

'Why? Take a look in the mirror and you'll see.' Linda sounded exasperated. 'Your trouble is that you don't realise just how gorgeous you are. If you knew how many men in this place have lusted after you, I'm sure you'd be shocked! No wonder Mike is cock-a-hoop that you're going to the Christmas dance with him.'

'You're exaggerating.' She frowned. 'I only agreed to go to the dance with Mike because I felt so guilty about us falling out. I hope he isn't reading too much into it.'

'I don't know about that but I'm sure it's given his standing in this place a bit of a boost. He's letting it be known that he's snatched you out from under dishy Daniel's nose!'

Emma was incensed to hear that. 'It wasn't like that at all! Daniel hasn't even asked me to go to the dance with him. I don't think he's even thought about going, with having Amy to look after.'

'You know that and I know that, but the rest of the people around here don't appear to,' Linda observed wryly. 'Maybe you should set Mike straight before Daniel hears the rumours. I still live in hope that you two will get your act together.'

Emma didn't say anything to that but she couldn't help wondering what she should do. It was wrong of Mike to go spreading stories like that. She decided to have a word with him as soon as she got the chance. Maybe it would be better if she didn't go to the dance after all, because it seemed to be causing no end of problems.

She had the opportunity to speak to him sooner than she'd expected. She was in the staffroom after lunch, combing her hair before going back on duty, when Mike came in and she decided that there was no time like the present to set matters straight.

'Can I have a word with you, Mike?'

'Sure. Any time, any place, anywhere,' he agreed, giving her a smile that set her teeth on edge. He laid a possessive arm around her shoulders and looked into her eyes. 'What is it, my sweet?'

Emma pointedly removed his arm. 'I believe that you've been telling everyone that you beat Daniel Hutton to it by getting me to agree to go to the dance with you.'

Mike shrugged. 'So what? It's more or less true, isn't it?'

'No, it isn't true. Daniel has never mentioned the dance to me. You're giving everyone entirely the wrong impression.'

'Oh, come on, Emma! What does it matter?' Mike grinned at her. 'If Daniel didn't ask you then I'm not treading on his toes, am I?'

'I still don't like the idea that you're turning this into something it isn't. I only agreed to go with you because I didn't want to refuse after you'd tried to make amends for what happened last week,' she retorted.

'Oh, did you?' Mike's face darkened. 'Well, it may interest you to know that I wasn't trying to make amends. I saw it as the perfect way to put Hutton's nose out of joint! I've had it up to here with his preaching, I can tell you!'

Emma felt sick. 'Then all I can say is thank heavens I found out what you were up to. Find yourself another partner, Mike, because I won't be going with you!'

Emma left the staffroom. She could feel herself trembling and had to stop when she reached the office to take a deep breath. Ridiculous though it was, she felt deeply hurt that Mike had tried to use her to score points off Daniel like that.

'Emma? Are you OK? Is something wrong?'

She hadn't realised that Daniel was in the office, using the phone, and jumped as he spoke. His face darkened into a scowl as he came to the door and took hold of her arm. He led her into the room and closed the door.

'Tell me what's been going on.'

'Nothing!' She gave a shrill little laugh which wouldn't have convinced anyone she was telling the truth. It certainly didn't convince Daniel because his mouth compressed.

'You're a rotten liar, Emma. I can see that you're upset and I want to know why.'

She shook her head. 'It's nothing, really—just something Mike said.'

'Humphreys?' His tone was grimmer than ever. Emma had never heard Daniel sound like that before and looked at him in surprise.

'Would I be wrong to suggest that whatever he said or did had something to do with me?' He must have seen from the way the colour swept up her face that he had been right because his expression turned even grimmer.

'I want to know what's been going on, Emma. I promise you that I won't do anything to embarrass you in front of Humphreys. If he's still concerned because you're helping me, there's an easy solution. I won't keep you to your promise to help me arrange Amy's Christmas if it's causing you problems in your personal life.'

'It isn't!' Emma was horrified that he should have imagined that. 'I've told you before that Mike isn't my boyfriend. He's just someone I work with.'

'So what's the problem, then? I can't understand if you won't explain.' Daniel sounded exasperated and Emma realised that she was just making the situation worse.

'Mike had a word with me the other day and asked me

if I would still go to the Christmas dance with him.' She shrugged, feeling uncomfortable about pouring the whole story out to Daniel. 'He told me that he was sorry that we'd fallen out and wanted us to be friends, and I believed him.'

'Only he had an ulterior motive for asking you?' Daniel smiled thinly. 'Why doesn't that surprise me?'

'Y-yes.' Emma rushed on, wanting to get it over with as quickly as possible. 'Evidently, Mike saw it as a way to get one over on you. If…if I was going to the dance with him then I couldn't go with you.' She tailed off, wondering if she should have told Daniel the truth or not. It was hard to tell because his expression revealed very little about his feelings.

'I see. I imagine the fact that you'd agreed to go with him would also have increased his standing amongst his friends.' He gave her a dry look. 'It's widely known that you're very discriminating when it comes to accepting dates, Emma.'

'It's a shame I wasn't discriminating in this case, then, wasn't it?' she replied, trying to lighten the mood. Daniel looked rather scary, she decided, studying the grim set of his mouth. That he was annoyed on her behalf went without saying, and her heart warmed at the thought that he cared about her being used by Mike for his own miserable ends.

'It was. Humphreys isn't fit to lick your boots,' he declared softly. Emma felt her heart leap into her throat as he looked at her. His eyes were lit by some inner fire yet she knew that it wasn't simply anger that made them glow that way. When he reached out and touched her cheek she felt her breath catch, though it had been the lightest of touches.

His voice seemed to have reached new depths as he added softly, 'Any man who earns your love, Emma, would be fortunate indeed.'

What might have happened next was anyone's guess. However, the sound of someone tapping on the door broke the spell and reminded them both of where they were.

'Come in.' Daniel swung round, his face smoothing into its customary noncommittal expression as Sister Carter came into the office with a message for him.

Emma excused herself and hurried back to the ward, but all afternoon she found her thoughts returning to what had happened—the way Daniel had looked at her and what he'd said. It felt as though something had changed in their relationship but she was too scared to let herself wonder what it might be. If she didn't think about it, maybe it would happen…whatever *it* was!

'Mike's been in a foul mood all afternoon. What did you say to him, Em?'

They were in the staffroom, collecting their coats at the end of the day, when Linda asked the question. Emma sighed but there was no reason why she should keep what had happened a secret from her friend.

She briefly explained what had gone on, without going into detail, and heard Linda sigh. 'Uh-oh! You'll have to watch out. Mike isn't a person I'd like to cross so be on your toes, Em. It won't sit easily with him when everyone finds out that you dumped him for Daniel.'

'But I didn't!' Emma protested.

'I know that, but that isn't how it will look to everyone else. You know how folk love a good gossip so they'll put their own spin on the story once it gets round. Mike isn't going to be a happy bunny so just watch your back. OK?'

Emma nodded miserably, wishing she could erase the whole unpleasant episode. It was going to be pretty miserable, working with Mike, if he was determined to pay her back. She hauled her coat out of her locker, glancing down as something dropped out of her pocket.

'Here you go… My, my, someone's in the money!' Linda grinned as she shoved a wad of ten-pound notes back into the envelope. Her brows rose as she turned it over and read the logo printed on the back. 'Wilkins Jewellers. What have you been doing, Em, selling the family silver?'

'How did you guess?' Emma laughed as she took the envelope from her friend and put it in her bag. It was the money Daniel had given her the previous night to buy the Christmas shopping—she'd forgotten about it being in her coat pocket.

She left it at that, not wanting to have to explain to Linda that Daniel had given it to her. It didn't feel right, discussing every detail of their arrangement with a third party, to be frank. Linda didn't mention it again as they left the hospital together. Emma had brought the hire car with her and her friend's brows rose when she saw it.

'A car as well? Forget the family silver—you must have won the lottery.' Linda looked round as her boyfriend, Gary, beeped his car horn. 'Have to go. It's the big day today. Gary's taking me into town to buy my engagement ring.'

'How lovely. Have fun!' Emma waved them off then got into the car. It was one of the latest models and it was a pleasure driving it, she thought as she set off for a supermarket on the outskirts of town. She rarely had the chance to go there to shop so it was a treat to be able to go that night. She had a list of everything she needed, food-wise, for Christmas and intended to get the bulk of it done so that she would have more time to spend looking for Amy's presents.

Armed with the list, she spent a couple of hours loading her trolley with goodies. The size of the bill made her blanch but she consoled herself with the thought that she would offer to split the cost of the food with Daniel. After all, she would be eating a lot of what she'd bought so it was only fair.

She left the supermarket and headed back towards town, pausing when she came to the junction. If she turned left she could be at Daniel's house within ten minutes. It would make more sense to take the shopping straight there.

Her heart lifted at the thought of seeing him again even if was only for a few minutes. She parked in front of his house then went and knocked on the door. He'd given her a key but there was no way that she wanted to use it when he was at home. It didn't seem right.

His face broke into a welcoming smile when he saw her. 'Emma! What a lovely surprise. Come in.'

'Actually, I've only called to bring the shopping,' she explained, warmed by his greeting.

'I'll fetch it inside. You go on in. Amy's in the sitting room. She'll be thrilled when she sees you.'

Daniel took the car keys from her and headed down the drive. Emma watched him walk to the car while a lump came to her throat. What a normal everyday kind of event, to arrive home with bags full of shopping. Millions of women—and men—performed the very same task week in and week out yet for her it was a special moment to treasure.

It was what being part of a family must be like—performing all the humdrum tasks and sharing them with someone else. It was a taste of a life she'd never known, a life she wanted so much she ached...

Or did she ache because it was Daniel she wanted, his life she wanted to be part of, his future she wanted to share?

Emma took a deep breath as he turned and smiled when he saw her standing on the step. Maybe there should have been bells ringing or rockets going off at that moment. That was how it happened in films when a woman discovered that she was in love.

There were no bells or rockets for her, however, just a boot full of shopping. It didn't make any difference, though. She was in love with Daniel. How funny to realise it at that moment. How sad not to be able to run out into the street and tell him. Until she knew how Daniel felt about her, there was no way she could run the risk of embarrassing him by declaring her feelings.

Emma went inside the house and her heart was brimming over with joy and sadness. Could Daniel ever love her? Did he ever wish that Christmas could last for ever so that she could be a permanent part of his life?

She just didn't know!

CHAPTER NINE

'EMMA!'

Amy came racing across the room. Emma forced away the lingering sadness as she hugged the little girl.

'What a greeting! It makes me doubly glad I came.'

'What was the first reason?' Daniel paused by the door, his arms loaded with carrier bags. He grinned wickedly when Emma looked blankly at him. 'You said that you were *doubly* glad that you came to visit us.'

Emma laughed, glad of the moment of lightness because it helped ease the ache inside her. 'Doctors can be very pedantic at times! If only their handwriting was as good as their grasp of the English language, eh?'

'Ouch! Not that it's answered my question, of course. If doctors are pedantic then nurses are very adept at prevaricating.' Daniel's eyes glinted with amusement and Emma smiled back at him.

'I dispute that. Nurses are just *tactful*. That's an entirely different thing. Anyway, Dr Pedantic, I meant that I was glad to come because it means you can unload all that shopping.'

He rolled his eyes. 'And here I was thinking you were pleased to see me.'

He carried on down the hall, mercifully sparing her the need to answer. Emma sighed, thinking to herself that if he knew how glad she was to see him that would definitely alter things! Daniel might want to run a mile if he knew how she really felt about him...

'Emma, you're not listening!'

She jolted back to the present as Amy shook her arm.

'I'm sorry, darling. I was wool-gathering. What did you say?'

'I was telling you that Uncle Daniel and I are going carol-singing tonight. Will you come with us, Emma? Please!'

'Oh, I'm not sure…' Emma sighed when she saw Amy's face fall. 'Let's see what Uncle Daniel says, shall we?'

Daniel had finished bringing in the shopping and was standing in the kitchen, staring bemusedly at the amount of goodies Emma had bought. He looked round and grinned when they came into the room.

'We could feed an army with this little lot!'

Emma flushed. 'I'm sorry. Maybe I have gone a bit over the top…' she began apologetically.

'Nonsense!' Daniel came round the table and hugged her. 'We wanted a Christmas with all the trimmings and that's what we're going to have. Anyway, we can always throw a party to use up any food we haven't eaten.'

Emma's heart sang as he included her in his plans so naturally. Maybe it was foolish to read too much into it but she couldn't help it. She loved him so much that the thought of having even an extra day with him was like being given a wonderful gift.

'Uncle Daniel, can Emma come carol-singing with us?'

Amy, with a child's eye for the priorities, returned the conversation to what was uppermost in her mind. Daniel shrugged, looking faintly surprised that she'd asked him such a question.

'Of course she can.' He released Emma and went to make a start on putting away the food. 'It's Amy's Sunday school class who are carol-singing, although there'll be lots of parents going along as well. Evidently, it's something of a tradition and Amy and Claire have always gone along. I thought it would be nice if we went this year, too.'

He picked up the turkey and stowed it carefully in the bottom of the—thankfully large—refrigerator. 'It would be great if you came as well, Emma. It would make it all the more special.'

Emma smiled, although she could feel the excitement coiling tightly in her stomach. There had been something in Daniel's voice when he'd said that, a note which had told her he'd meant it. Daniel wanted her to go with them that night and not just because it would please Amy.

'Then I'd love to come.'

'Good.' The smile Daniel gave her was so gentle that it brought a lump to her throat.

'Yes!' Amy's shout of pleasure cut short the moment. Emma took a small breath before she turned to the excited child.

'Let's help Uncle Daniel get all this shopping put away then we can get ready.'

Amy set to with great gusto. With the three of them working together, it didn't take long to fill the fridge and freezer, not to mention the cupboards. Daniel folded up the plastic carriers and stowed them in a drawer then sent Amy upstairs to fetch her coat.

'Have you got a scarf with you, Emma? It will get cold out there tonight. Did you know that they're forecasting snow in the next twenty-four hours?'

'Really? Oh, wouldn't it be marvellous if we had a white Christmas? It would make it extra-special!'

'It's going to be extra-special with or without the snow.' Daniel caught her hand and pulled her towards him. His hazel eyes shimmered as he looked into her face. 'This is going to be the best Christmas ever, Emma—for all of us.'

His lips were warm as they closed over hers. Emma simply gave herself up to the pleasure of having him kiss her. When he drew back there was a faintly bemused expression on his face but, then, she guessed that there was a matching one on hers!

'I suppose we'd better go and get ready,' he suggested with such reluctance that she couldn't help smiling.

'I suppose we should.'

Daniel's grin was a trifle crooked as he raised her hand to his mouth and kissed her fingertips. 'You're the best thing that could have happened to me and Amy. I want you to know that.'

'Thank you.' She managed to smile, although she could feel the emotions welling inside her. Maybe it was foolish to let herself get carried away but she couldn't help hoping that he meant that in the way she wanted him to.

Amy came clattering down the stairs just then, her coat all askew, her hat rammed down over her eyebrows. Emma chuckled as she set about sorting her out and soon had the little girl ready to leave the house.

'Here, put this on.' Daniel wound a thick, cherry-red woollen scarf around Emma's neck. He made sure that it was snugly fastened to keep out the cold air then drew her hood over her head. 'I don't want you getting cold tonight.'

Emma smiled because her heart was overflowing with happiness. Nobody had ever taken such care of her as Daniel did. She stepped out onto the path and looked up at the frosty sky. There were a lot of stars out that night and one in particular was very bright.

She closed her eyes and made a wish, wondering if there was any truth in the saying about wishes coming true if you wished on a star. She hoped so. She really did. She didn't want to lose what she had at this moment. She wanted it to go on and on for ever!

'I'm afraid this will have to be our last performance, every-one.' The vicar smiled as there was a chorus of groans. 'I know. It's been a wonderful evening. Thank you all for coming.'

'It has been fun, hasn't it?' Daniel grinned at Emma as the band of carol-singers headed down the road. 'I can't remember when I last went carol-singing, can you?'

'I can't.' Emma clutched hold of the songsheet as the

wind tried to whip it out of her hands. It was difficult to hold onto it because she was wearing a pair of thick woolly mittens. She looked up in surprise when something plopped onto the paper. 'It's snowing!'

Daniel laughed. 'So it is! Wowee!'

He sounded all of ten years old at that moment and Emma couldn't help laughing. 'No one would ever believe that you were usually so poised. There are two sides to you, Daniel Hutton, did you know that?'

'I refuse to answer on the grounds that it might incriminate me,' he declared loftily. Whipping the errant songsheet out of her hand, he took hold of it instead. 'Come along now. No loitering. Our superb voices are needed.'

Emma chuckled as he led her down the street to where the group had assembled outside some bungalows. The area was part of the town's sheltered housing scheme for elderly people and one of the regular ports of call on the yearly carol-singing route. Emma could see that most of the old folk were standing in their windows, watching.

Daniel made space for her beside him with the rest of the adult singers. Amy and the other children were gathered at the front. The vicar had brought along a lantern and the scene was like something from a Christmas card, Emma thought as she looked at the children's smiling faces in the lamplight.

The snow was coming down harder now, turning the pavements and gardens white. She stuck out her tongue and caught an icy snowflake on the tip of it then smiled at her own childishness. She glanced at Daniel to see if he'd seen how silly she was being and felt her heart stop when she saw the expression in his eyes. Obviously, Daniel didn't think it had been at all childish…

It was an effort to concentrate as the vicar announced the first carol and everyone began to sing. However, Emma was soon caught up in the singing. One carol flowed on to another as they worked their way through the whole repertoire and ended with the ever-beautiful 'Silent Night'.

Emma knew that she wasn't the only one who was sorry when they finished and the vicar announced that it was time to go home. It had been a magical, wonderful night and one she would remember for ever.

'Right, time to go home, sprog.' Daniel lifted a tired Amy into his arms as they walked back up the street. The little girl snuggled against him, yawning.

'It was fun, Uncle Daniel. Just like when Mummy and I used to go carol-singing. I know Mummy's in heaven but d'you think she knows what we've been doing tonight?'

Daniel smiled at Emma over the top of his niece's head and Emma could see the sadness in his eyes. 'I'm sure she does, sweetheart. I bet she's really pleased that you had a lovely time, too.'

'Spect so,' Amy said trustingly. She snuggled closer to Daniel, her eyelids drooping. She was asleep by the time they reached the end of the road and didn't wake until they arrived home.

'Here, I've got a key.' Emma quickly unlocked the door because Daniel was hampered by the child in his arms.

'Thanks. Look, I'll take Amy straight up to bed. I won't be long. Will you wait, Emma?'

For ever! she wanted to say, but merely nodded. 'Shall I make us a drink? Tea or coffee perhaps?'

'Whichever you prefer.' Daniel gave her a quick smile before he carried Amy upstairs.

Emma went into the kitchen and took off her coat and scarf, draping them over the back of a chair. She filled the kettle then stared out of the window. The snow lent the garden a fairy-like prettiness. It was that kind of night when there seemed to be magic in the air—unless it was just how she was feeling.

She felt a bubble of excitement floating beneath the surface of her mind, a frisson of anticipation as though something wonderful was going to happen. She could sense it, feel it, and it both scared and exhilarated her. When Daniel came into the kitchen she didn't turn round because she was afraid that the bubble would burst and she didn't want that to happen yet.

'Emma?'

He said her name softly, questioningly, and she had to turn, though it took her a moment to find the courage. She loved him so much that it seemed to drain the strength from her limbs as it hit her how empty her life would be without him in the future.

'Emma.' He said her name again, softer still, aching with tenderness, throbbing with passion. It seemed that she'd never heard the word before, never known that it could sound that way—so beautiful, so full of emotion.

Her eyes lifted to his face, caught by the myriad emotions she could see on it. Maybe she should have tried to decipher them but she didn't have the strength. It was easier to stand there while Daniel took a couple of steps until he was so close that she could touch him.

His body felt warm and hard as she laid her hand against his chest, so vital and alive that Emma murmured yet she wasn't aware of making any sound. She could feel the rhythmic beating of his heart beneath her palm, feel the tremor which ran through him all of a sudden. He said her name again, softly yet with a need in his voice which made an answering yearning awake inside her. She was already moving towards him when he pulled her into his arms.

Their bodies met with a small jolt, like the aftershock of a huge seismic eruption, even though nothing had gone before. Daniel's mouth was hungry as it claimed hers, but hers was just as greedy. There was nothing poised about this kiss, nothing practised or perfect about the urgent meeting of their mouths. Their desire for each other was too raw to worry about polish and performance. Daniel wanted her and she wanted him. That was all that mattered.

He was breathing heavily when he raised his head. 'Tell me now if this isn't want you want, Emma.'

She heard the roughness in his voice and knew how hard it had been for him to stop when what he'd wanted had been to carry on. That was what she wanted, too—to lose herself in this passion, to lose herself in Daniel. It touched her heart and her soul to know how much he cared about her feelings.

'I do want it, though, Daniel.' She went on tiptoe, punctuating her words with kisses, feeling his heart racing almost out of control as it beat against her breasts. 'I…want…it more…than…'

She didn't get chance to finish. She didn't need to. Daniel knew what she was telling him. He drew her back into his arms and his eyes blazed.

'You won't ever regret this, Emma. I promise you that!'

Emma closed her eyes, letting the words sink deep into her soul. She wanted to believe them so much and maybe she should. There had been magic in the air tonight so maybe wishes could come true.

Daniel kissed her again, his mouth drawing a response from her that Emma hadn't known herself capable of. Her body felt as though it were on fire, the blood almost too hot as it flowed through her veins. She was trembling when the kiss ended but so was Daniel. He cupped her face between his hands as he stared into her eyes, and his voice was so husky that she *felt* as much as heard the words he ground out.

'Will you stay the night with me, Emma?'

'Yes.' Oddly, her own voice sounded so normal that she smiled. Funny that on such a momentous occasion she could feel so confident and carefree. But maybe it wasn't strange when she thought about it. She loved Daniel so showing him how she felt was the most natural thing in the world.

He kissed her once more then took hold of her hand and

led her upstairs to his bedroom. Emma looked round the drably painted room and smiled. 'Beige again.'

He laughed softly as he closed the door then came up behind her and slid his arms around her waist so that he could nuzzle her neck. 'The colour my life was until you came and brightened it up, Emma.'

She smiled at that, letting her head fall to the side as his mouth worked its way towards the curve of her ear. 'You have a nice line in patter, Dr Hutton,' she teased him.

'You think so?' He turned her round to face him and the expression in his eyes made her breath catch. 'Maybe you should sample some action next. I wouldn't want you thinking that I was all talk...'

He didn't quite finish the sentence as his desire got the better of him. Emma murmured incoherently as his mouth claimed hers in a drugging kiss which seemed to steal her ability to think. Why think when you can feel, anyway? her heart murmured, and she took its advice.

Daniel's hands moved to the hem of her sweater so that he could draw it over her head. He tossed it aside with barely a glance because his eyes were locked to what it had revealed. Emma felt her nipples harden as his eyes ran over her full breasts, barely concealed by the lacy black bra she was wearing.

'You're beautiful, Emma, very, very beautiful...'

He trailed a finger almost reverently over the full curve of one breast. Emma bit her lip to contain her gasp of pleasure but somehow it still escaped from her lips. The excitement she had felt before seemed to have increased tenfold so that she was trembling with it...

Or perhaps the truth was that she was trembling with desire. She had never felt like this before so she couldn't judge and didn't try. It was enough to know that Daniel wanted her and that what she saw in his eyes was for her and her alone. Even if Daniel couldn't love her for ever she knew in her heart that he loved her at that moment!

'Emma. Sweet, beautiful Emma.'

She went into his arms willingly, trustingly, knowing that whatever happened later she would never regret what was happening now…

The light was so bright that Emma had to shade her eyes. She looked round the unfamiliar room, at the light pouring in through the window, and frowned. It took her a moment to remember where she was and her heart lurched as she realised that she was in Daniel's bed.

She rolled onto her side, feeling the flurry which ran through her as her thigh brushed his. He was still asleep, his long lashes painting shadows on his cheeks, his breathing slow and steady.

Emma smiled as she lay there absorbing all the tiny details, like how a night's growth of beard had darkened his jawbone, how the tiny lines that fanned from the corners of his eyes were so much paler than the rest of his skin. It was what an artist had to do before he painted a portrait—absorb the details, fine-tune his mind to assimilate the insignificant as well as the more important features.

She already knew how Daniel looked—if she'd had the skill she could have painted his portrait from memory without any trouble. But it wouldn't have had all the minuscule details that would have made it true to life. She wanted to store up all those details, build up in her mind a complete picture of this man she loved…

'I'm getting a complex, lying here. You *do* remember who I am, I hope?'

She jumped, the colour sweeping up her cheeks when she realised that Daniel was watching her from under his lashes. He gave a deep laugh as he rolled onto his side and propped himself up on his elbow.

'You seemed so intent when you were looking at me that I was beginning to wonder if you'd forgotten my name.'

Emma laughed because it was impossible not to find his teasing funny. 'Not at all. It's David, isn't it?'

'It most certainly isn't!' He clamped a strong arm around her waist and scooped her towards him so fast that she didn't have time to draw breath. 'Think you can tease me like that and get away with it, do you?'

His punishment was a very thorough kiss, which left Emma reeling. Daniel looked decidedly smug when he saw her expression. 'So, what's my name, woman?'

'Daniel…' She cleared her throat and repeated it. 'Daniel.'

'That's better!' Rolling onto his back, he drew her into the crook of his arm and his tone was gentle all of a sudden. 'Are you OK, Emma?'

She knew what he meant and nodded, feeling her cheek rubbing against his warm skin. 'I'm fine.'

He turned to look at her and his eyes were dark, questioning. 'No regrets? Honestly?'

'None.' She took a deep breath then plucked up her courage. 'How about you, Daniel? H-have you any regrets?'

'No. I—' He broke off as the sound of footsteps pattering along the landing alerted him to the fact that Amy was awake. Sudden indecision crossed his face and Emma knew at once that he was concerned about his niece's reaction if she discovered them in bed together.

'Why don't you get Amy ready for school?' she suggested softly, not wanting to cause problems for him. 'I'll pop into the spare bedroom so that Amy will think I spent the night there.'

'You don't mind?' Daniel frowned. 'I just don't want Amy getting the wrong idea, you understand. Children are so impressionable, aren't they?'

Emma nodded, although a dull little ache crept into her heart as she wondered what kind of *wrong* impression his niece would have received. Was he afraid that Amy might think that Emma was going to be a permanent addition to their lives? And was that something he didn't foresee happening? Suddenly she was awash with doubts so that it was hard to maintain her smile.

Daniel seemed not to sense that she was upset, thankfully enough. Snatching up the robe from the end of the bed, he dragged it on then smiled at her. 'Thanks, Emma. For everything.'

He hurried from the room but it was a few seconds before Emma could force herself to get up. She shivered as she dragged on her clothes then quickly straightened the rumpled bed. Why had Daniel thanked her like that? Because she'd stayed the night with him?

The thought was another black cloud on her bright horizon so that her happy mood slowly dissipated. What might have meant the world to her might not have meant nearly so much to Daniel. She had to face that now. Just because she loved him, it didn't mean that he felt anything for her.

Amy was eating breakfast when Emma went down to the kitchen ten minutes later. The little girl smiled when she saw her, although she didn't appear surprised.

'Hello, Emma. Uncle Daniel said that you were asleep so I had to be quiet,' she explained, spooning cereal into her mouth.

'You were like a little mouse!' Emma gave the little girl a hug then glanced round as Daniel picked up the teapot.

'Fancy a cup? There's toast as well.'

She shook her head, not wanting to prolong what was turning into an awkward situation, or at least it was awkward for her. Daniel didn't appear at all fazed by it, she noted, and that thought made it hurt all the more.

'No, thanks. I'd better get a move on or I'll be late for work.'

She headed for the door but Daniel was right behind her. 'I'll see you out.'

He followed her down the hall, politely taking her coat

off the hook and holding it out for her. However, when Emma tried to move away his hands clasped her shoulders.

'I get the distinct impression that something has upset you, Emma.'

She shook her head. 'Don't be silly. Of course I'm not upset. Why should I be?'

He turned her to face him. 'Because this isn't the way last night should have ended. It isn't how I would choose to have it end, believe me. But I won't do anything that might…well, might upset Amy. Where she's concerned, I have to be one hundred per cent certain that what I am doing is right.'

There was an odd note in his voice but Emma barely noticed it. Her mind had homed in on the thought that Daniel didn't believe it was *right* to have her in his life! Somehow she managed to conceal her pain because it was unthinkable to let him know how hurt she was when that had never been his intention.

'I'm sure you're right, Daniel. Amy's welfare must be your main priority.'

His eyes darkened. 'It is. I won't do anything that might cause her more pain. Amy's had enough heartache in her young life as it is.'

There wasn't anything Emma could say to that. In her heart she knew that he was right to take such a stand. However, it didn't make her feel better to know how easily he could cut her out of his life.

She gave him a quick smile, aware that tears were only a blink away from falling. 'I'd better be off. I'm not due in till eleven today but there are things I need to do.'

'I've got meetings most of the day so I doubt if I'll see you.' Daniel sighed. 'With Max off I'm having to stand in for him and it isn't easy, trying to do things the way he would do them. I'm very much aware that I could be treading on his toes if I'm not careful.'

'Tricky situation, but I'm sure you'll do what you think best,' Emma said lightly.

'Mmm, but best for one person might not be best for another,' he replied quietly.

She didn't ask him to explain that rather cryptic remark as she hurried out to the car. There were many ways to interpret it. Daniel might have considered it a good idea to ask her to help him give Amy a wonderful Christmas but it might not be *his* idea of the best way to spend it.

Emma closed her mind to that unhappy thought as she made her way up the path. There was a thick layer of snow on the ground and more snow still falling, making it difficult to keep her footing. She hunted her keys out of her pocket and unlocked the car then glanced round when Daniel called out to her.

'Drive carefully, Emma.'

It was an effort to smile as she got into the car. Emma's hand shook as she started the engine. She knew that in years to come she would picture him standing there at the door. Her mind had taken a mental snapshot of the scene. It was one more memory to add to all the memories they'd made the previous night, something to look back on when Daniel was no longer part of her life. It seemed all too little to ward off the loneliness of the coming years.

Emma arrived at the hospital just before eleven. She was heading for the staffroom to change into her uniform when Sister Carter stopped her.

'Emma, can you come into the office, please? The police are here and they'd like a word with you about Paula's ring.'

'It hasn't turned up, then?' Emma sighed when Sister Carter shook her head. 'Oh, dear.'

She went straight to the office where she was interviewed by the two policemen, who wanted to know exactly what had happened the day Paula had been admitted. Emma repeated what she'd told Sister Carter then left the office. However, the nagging feeling that maybe she was a suspect didn't sit easily with her. It wasn't nice to know that anyone would think she was capable of such a horrible deed.

Linda was working the late shift as well that day and had been delayed because of the snow. She came rushing into the ward almost half an hour after the time she should have been there.

'The buses were cancelled along my route so Gary had to take the car this morning. I was hoping they'd be running again by the time I left, but no such luck. I ended up having to walk, and it took me ages!'

Emma smiled sympathetically. 'What a drag! You should have phoned me and I could have picked you up.'

'I'd forgotten about you having transport. Drat!' Linda rolled her eyes as she stopped beside Paula Walters's bed. 'I think you must have a money tree at home, Em. Between that envelope full of tenners and a new car!'

Emma laughed. 'If only! No, Dan—' She broke off as Paula suddenly let out a shriek and turned to her in alarm. 'Paula, are you all right?'

'That's my ring! She's wearing my ring!'

Emma's mouth dropped open as she realised that Paula was pointing at Linda. It was only then that she realised her friend was wearing an obviously expensive sapphire and diamond engagement ring.

'I don't know what you're talking about!' Linda looked horrified. 'Gary and I bought this ring last night at the jeweller's in town.'

She turned appealingly to Emma. 'You remember me saying that we were going in to town to buy my engagement ring, don't you? We bought it from Wilkins, that jeweller's in the high street.'

'It's my ring! I know it is.' Paula was becoming more and more agitated. 'Stephen had it made specially for me. I have the designer's drawings at home so I can prove it!'

Both women were obviously upset and no wonder. When Sister Carter came hurrying from the office to see what was going on, Emma quickly explained. Sister decided that she had no option but to call the police and asked Linda to wait in her office until they arrived.

The police arrived a short time later and took a statement from Linda. They also took away the ring, which upset her even more. Paula's fiancé had been summoned and he, too, had identified it as being the ring he'd had made for her. He'd brought with him the designer's drawings and they seemed to prove that the ring was the one that had gone missing from Paula's bag.

Between trying to console Linda and keep the ward running smoothly, Emma had little time to think properly. It was a relief when it was time to go home because the atmosphere in the ward had been dreadful all day long.

Emma breathed a sigh of relief as she let herself into her flat. With a bit of luck everything would have been sorted out by the following day and they could get back to normal. Although how the ring had ended up in the jeweller's possession was anyone's guess. Still, there had to be a logical explanation for it.

It was another late shift the following day, the last one before her Christmas break. It was busy as usual so that Emma was glad when break-time came around. Linda had been very subdued at first but she cheered up as the day had worn on. Gary had phoned to say that he'd been to the police station with the receipt and the police now accepted that the ring had been bought in good faith, which was something to be thankful for.

Of course, the story had spread like wildfire through the hospital. However, it wasn't until break-time that Emma realised the full extent of the rumours that were circulating when she happened to overhear two nurses from a different ward talking while she was in the ladies' cloakroom.

'Evidently, the finger is pointing at Emma Graham,' one

nurse told the other, unaware that Emma was in one of the stalls. 'I heard that she was the only one who knew that the ring was in the woman's bag. Obviously, she was ideally placed to take it.'

'I know. I didn't want to believe it at first. I mean, Emma, of all people! But then I heard that she had all that money in an envelope with the jeweller's name on it.' The second nurse sighed. 'It does seem suspicious, doesn't it…?'

Emma didn't hear the rest of their conversation as the two women left the cloakroom. She didn't want to. What she'd heard already made her feel sick. Where on earth had those ugly rumours sprung from? She couldn't believe that Linda was responsible but someone must have started them.

Her heart lurched painfully. What would Daniel think when he heard them? Would he believe them? If people she'd worked with for several years were ready to think so badly of her then surely he would have doubts?

She felt her eyes fill with tears and angrily brushed them away. What Daniel believed was up to him but she had to put a stop to what was being said!

She left the cloakroom and hurried back to the ward. Her heart seemed to lurch to a stop when she got out of the lift and saw Daniel and the two policemen standing by the office. He turned when he heard her footsteps and his face was set into such a grimly uncompromising expression that she shivered. Daniel was angry, very angry indeed, but who with? Her? Surely he couldn't believe that she was capable of stealing from a patient?

'Would you come into the office, please, Emma?' he asked her flatly. 'The police need to speak to you about Paula's ring.'

Emma took a deep breath but it felt as though something inside her had just died. It would make no difference even if she proved her innocence. To know that Daniel didn't have enough faith in her to *know* that she wasn't guilty was too much to bear!

CHAPTER TEN

THE next half-hour was a nightmare. Emma repeated what she'd told the police the previous day. She was aware that Daniel was sitting at one side of the room, listening to every word. She glanced at him but there was nothing in his face to tell her what he was thinking.

The senior of the two police officers checked his notes. 'Mr Wilkins from the jeweller's has given us a description of the young woman who sold him the ring. He describes her as being in her early twenties, of medium height, with short blond hair.' The policeman looked up.

'Obviously, there must be a lot of young women who fit that description in this town, Miss Graham. However, it has been brought to our attention that you had in your possession quite a considerable sum of money in an envelope bearing the jeweller's name and address. Can you explain where you got it from?'

'I think I can answer that question, sergeant.' Daniel's expression was grimmer than ever as the two policemen looked questioningly at him. Emma took a deep breath but the feeling of sickness didn't go away. Even if Daniel explained about the money and the police believed him, it wouldn't alter the fact that he'd believed her capable of theft.

'Miss Graham kindly agreed to help me with the preparations for Christmas. I withdrew three hundred pounds from my bank account on Monday and gave it to her to pay for the shopping and various other items that I'd asked her to buy.'

'I see.' The policeman frowned. 'I imagine that you must have a record of this cash withdrawal?'

'Certainly. And I'm sure my bank will be happy to verify it as well,' Daniel confirmed.

'How did you happen to have one of the jeweller's envelopes in your possession, Dr Hutton? I am assuming that it was you who put the money in the envelope?' the policeman queried.

'It was. Whilst I was in town, withdrawing the cash, I went into the jeweller's to collect an item of jewellery that was being repaired. Mr Wilkins wrapped it in one of his envelopes. I had the envelope in my pocket and put the money into it before I gave it to Miss Graham. I'm sure that Mr Wilkins will be able to confirm that as well.'

Daniel's tone was clipped, as though he resented being cross-questioned about his actions. Would that be another point against her? Emma wondered sadly. The fact that Daniel had been dragged into this unpleasant affair? He would be bound to resent it, and resent her for causing him all this trouble.

Her spirits had sunk so low that they didn't rise even when the policeman closed his notebook. 'Well, that seems to have cleared up a few points. I'm sorry to have troubled you, Miss Graham. I hope you understand that we have to follow up every lead we get.'

Emma forced herself to smile as the two policemen got up to leave. 'I understand. I wish that I could have been more help but I have no idea who took Paula's ring.'

'Before you go, sergeant, you mentioned something about being given a lead. Was it someone from the hospital who contacted you?' Daniel asked, standing up as well.

Emma frowned, wondering what he wanted to know that for.

The sergeant shrugged. 'I'm afraid that I'm not at liberty to say, sir. I'm sure you understand.'

He nodded politely to them then left. Emma stood up as the two officers disappeared. She saw Daniel look at her but she didn't look at him in case he saw the hurt in her eyes. It felt as though her heart had been ripped apart to know that he'd suspected her even if it had been only for a few minutes.

'I'd better get back to work,' she murmured, hurrying to the door.

'Emma, wait! Look, I think we need to talk about this, don't you?' he began, but she didn't let him finish.

'No. Quite frankly, I can't see that there's anything to talk about! I'm only sorry that you didn't feel able to trust me, Daniel.'

'What do you mean?' He sounded so stunned that for a moment her foolish heart grasped at the idea that she'd made a mistake. But she'd seen the look on his face, hadn't she? What further proof did she need?

'You know what I mean. At the very least I would have expected you to give me the benefit of the doubt before you found me guilty of stealing Paula's ring! Still, why should you have done that when the rest of the staff in this hospital evidently believe that I'm a thief?'

'Emma…!'

She didn't wait to hear what he had to say. She didn't want to hear it. It was easy to apologise after the event but that didn't change a thing. Daniel should have *known* in his heart that she wasn't capable of stealing the ring!

Emma went back to the ward, feeling as though she were weighed down by despair. When Linda came hurrying over to ask what the police had wanted, she flatly explained.

'Someone tipped them off that you had that money? I hope you don't think it was me, Em,' Linda exclaimed in horror. 'It never crossed my mind that you had anything to do with Paula's ring going missing. You wouldn't do a thing like that!'

'I'm glad someone believes in me,' Emma said with a shrug when Linda looked at her. She didn't want to bring Daniel's name into the conversation because it was too painful.

'I overheard a couple of nurses talking about what had gone on. It appears that a lot of people in this hospital believe I'm the thief. They've heard about the money and put two and two together, it appears.'

'No!' Linda looked really upset. 'Oh, me and my big mouth. Why on earth did I mention it? It was just a joke, honestly. I made some crack about you being loaded. Everyone just laughed and I thought no more about it. I'm sorry, Emma. Really, I am.'

'It isn't your fault. Someone must have become suspicious and contacted the police. I suppose they thought it was the right thing to do.'

'But that's horrible! I can't remember exactly who was there when I was telling the tale, but to imagine one of your friends grassing on you like that is just awful!'

Emma laughed hollowly. 'Not really a friend, I'd say.'

They let the subject drop after that. Emma guessed that Linda was feeling guilty about her unwitting part in the events. All she could hope was that word would soon get around about her having been cleared by the police. However, that didn't compensate for the fact that Daniel had believed her guilty even if it had been only fleetingly.

It made Emma realise that there was no way that they could continue with their present arrangement. She made up her mind to explain that she wouldn't be able to help him after all as soon as she got a chance, but he didn't return to the ward as the afternoon wore on.

Shirley Rogers was being discharged that day and two of her sons arrived to collect her in the middle of the afternoon. Shirley hugged Emma before she left.

'Thank you for everything, love. I know it's probably not the right thing to say, but I've rather enjoyed being here!'

Emma laughed. 'Not many of our patients say that! Anyway, look after yourself, Shirley.' She turned to Shirley's eldest son, Martin, a strapping young man in his twenties. 'Don't go letting your mother do too much, will you?'

'No chance of that.' Martin winked at his brother. 'Ma is banned from the kitchen for the next month. We've set up a rota and got it all worked out as to who will be doing the cooking. Mind you, it's a test of endurance when it's Dad's turn. I never knew that you could make gravy so thick that you have to chew it!'

They all laughed. Shirley wiped her eyes as she let her son help her to her feet. 'The mind boggles at the thought of their dad cooking a meal. It will be the first time he's done it in thirty years of married life!'

'It just shows how much he cares, then, doesn't it, Shirley?' Emma said softly so that Shirley's sons couldn't hear.

'It does indeed. When you find a good man like my Ron, you're surely blessed.'

Emma smiled a little sadly to herself as Shirley left the ward with her sons. Shirley was right—it was a blessing to find a man who loved and cared for you for all those years. She couldn't help thinking about Daniel at that point before she realised how fruitless it was. Daniel wasn't going to be part of her life for much longer so there was no point in thinking about him in that context.

The day finally came to an end and Emma was glad when eight o'clock came around so that she could go home. It wasn't just the late shift or the amount of work she'd done which had left her feeling so tired. She was so dispirited by what had happened that day that it had cast a pall over everything.

It had stopped snowing but the night was very cold. A thick layer of frozen snow crunched beneath her feet as she made her way to the hire car. She got in, thinking how good it was to be able to drive home, instead of waiting at the bus stop on a night like this, although she wouldn't be able to enjoy such luxury for much longer.

She would phone Daniel in the morning before he left for work and explain that she'd decided that it would be better if they cancelled their arrangements for Christmas. Naturally, she would tell him to ask the garage to collect the car. She felt guilty about letting him down at the last minute but it would be for the best.

It didn't take Emma long to drive home. She parked outside her flat and got out of the car. She was halfway across the pavement before she saw the man standing by her front door. She came to a stop, wondering what Daniel was doing there at that time of the night.

'Hello, Emma. I know it's late but we need to talk.' He held up his hand when she opened her mouth. 'I know what you're going to say but I intend to get this cleared up right now. I'm willing to stand here all night if need be but I won't go away until you've heard what I have to say.'

'You'd better come in, then.' Emma walked stiffly up the path and unlocked the door. She simply didn't have the heart to argue with him. It would be easier to let him say his piece and then tell him what she'd decided.

She led the way up to her flat and let them in. The central heating was on but the air felt chilly. Leading the way into the living room, she lit the gas fire, aware that she was simply putting off the moment when Daniel would tell her why he'd come.

Did he want to tell her that he no longer needed her help? The thought was painful, even though she'd been going to tell him that she didn't think she would be able to help him any longer.

She swung round to confront him, not wanting to draw out the agony any longer. 'Look, Daniel, I'm tired so if you have something to say, please, get on with it.'

His mouth thinned. 'Very well. Obviously, you believe that I thought you'd stolen Paula's ring. Well, you're wrong. It never crossed my mind that you were responsible for it going missing!'

'No?' She gave a sceptical laugh. 'Come on, Daniel. I saw your face when I stepped out of that lift. You were angry, and the reason for it was because you were worried that you might have invited a thief into your life!'

'Yes, I *was* angry. But it certainly wasn't because I thought you were a thief.' His hazel eyes blazed as he glared at her. 'I was furious that anyone in his right mind should have imagined that you would do such a thing, Emma!'

'Oh!' She stared at him in confusion and heard him sigh roughly.

'Look, I may as well be honest and admit that I'd heard the rumours that were going around about you being involved in the theft of the ring. That was bad enough. However, until the police questioned you, I had no idea that I was partly responsible for them. If I hadn't given you that envelope full of money, there would have been no reason for people to start speculating.'

She heard the agony in his voice and knew that he was blaming himself for what had happened. 'It wasn't your fault, Daniel. I don't suppose it was anybody's fault, really. People just added two and two and came up with the wrong answer.'

'Maybe. Although those rumours must have started somewhere. Also, someone must have contacted the police and given them your name, otherwise they wouldn't have interviewed you.'

Emma shrugged, although it wasn't pleasant to imagine that someone she worked with had contacted the police even if it had been with the very best of intentions. 'Perhaps they felt they had to tell the police what they knew.'

'Perhaps.' Daniel suddenly sighed. 'I suppose you're right but I doubt that I could be so forgiving in your shoes, Emma.'

'So long as people accept that I'm not to blame then that's all I care about.' She hesitated but there was something she had to say, despite how difficult it was. 'Look, Daniel, I'll understand if you would prefer to forget about Christmas.'

'What do you mean—forget about it?'

'It's just that it may be, well, awkward for you, having your name linked with mine at the moment.' She gave a short laugh, trying to make light of it all. 'You know how mud sticks, and I certainly wouldn't want you getting a bad name as well as me!'

'Don't be daft!' He took hold of her hands and gave her a gentle shake. 'I don't care a jot what people are saying, Emma. I know that you're innocent. And I most certainly don't intend to spoil our wonderful Christmas because of malicious gossip.'

She felt tears fill her eyes and looked away, but not quickly enough. He drew her into his arms and held her tight. 'Oh, Emma, don't let it upset you. It really isn't worth crying over. Give it a couple of days and then all the gossip will have died down. Anyway, your friends know that you wouldn't have stolen Paula's ring and that's what matters.'

He tilted her face up and kissed her gently. His lips lingered for one second…two…

He sighed as he reluctantly drew back. 'I wish I could stay longer and convince you that none of this makes a scrap of difference, but I have to get back. I asked a neighbour to sit with Amy so that I could come here and I don't want to be gone too long.'

He gave her a last kiss then set her away from him. 'Anyway, the other reason I came was to ask you if you would do me the honour of being my partner at the dance tomorrow. I know it's short notice but I didn't think I'd be able to go. However, Amy has been invited to a sleep-over party at her friend's house so it means that I have a whole evening to myself. So will you come, Emma? Please.'

'Are you sure?' she began, but he interrupted her firmly. 'Quite sure. So if you're still worrying about what people are saying then forget it. We're going out on the town to-morrow and we're going to do it in style!'

Emma laughed at that. 'Mmm, you haven't been to a staff dance before, have you?' she teased. 'It's usually a lot of fun but as for stylish... Well, you'll see what I mean soon enough. I hope you're good at silly party games.'

'I'll soon learn if I'm not! Does that mean you'll come?' He grinned when she nodded. 'Great! The dance starts at seven so I'll pick you up at a quarter to if that's OK?'

'Fine.' She paused then hurried on. 'And you still want me to help with the Christmas arrangements, Daniel?'

He kissed her quickly. 'Yes! So stop worrying. This Christmas is going to be the best one we've ever had!'

He left straight after that. Emma sighed as she took off her coat. It might be the *best* Christmas ever but once it was over then that would be that. Daniel had made no mention of what would happen afterwards.

The next day flew by. Emma drove into Bournemouth and spent several hours shopping for presents for Amy. Top of her list was the Barbie doll with its sparkly dress. She added several other items to her basket, including a jigsaw puzzle in the shape of a pot-bellied pig—which was sure to appeal to the little girl—some colourful crayons and a thick pad of artist's paper.

She was flagging by the time one o'clock came round so she headed for a well-known department store which fronted the town's square. It was full of shoppers and the mood was very up-beat. Christmas songs were playing softly in the background and every department had been decorated with tinsel and baubles.

Emma made her way to the café on the top floor, stopping off on the way to visit the children's department where she bought a sweater for Amy in a lovely shade of blue. It struck her that she hadn't bought anything for Daniel as yet so she wandered through the homeware department, looking for something that would appeal to him. She didn't want to buy him anything too personal and decided that it might be better to give him something for the house.

The department was beautifully set out with arrangements of glass and china, silver and linen. It was hard to decide but in the end Emma opted for a glass paperweight which he would be able to use at home or in his office. It was quite expensive but she knew that Daniel would love the twisting patterns of purple and black glass embedded in it.

It was almost five when she arrived home so she just made herself a cup of tea, conscious of the fact that she had to get ready. Daniel would be arriving to collect her in less than two hours' time and she was going to need every minute to prepare!

Almost two hours later, Emma stood in front of the mirror and studied her reflection. It was the moment of truth. Would Daniel think that she looked all right?

Her eyes swept over her gleaming blond hair. She had decided on a new style that night but it suited her, she decided. With the silky strands tucked behind her ears she looked far more sophisticated than she usually did. She didn't have much jewellery but the sparkling diamanté studs she wore in her earlobes caught the light whenever she moved her head.

Her usual light make-up had been enhanced by shimmery face powder which gave her skin an added glow. Soft grey eye shadow and daringly black mascara made her eyes look huge and rather mysterious, while the plum-toned lipstick she'd bought in the summer sales and never dared wear before made her full mouth look little short of luscious.

Her increasingly confident gaze moved to her new black dress. As soon as she'd seen it in the window of that high-class boutique that afternoon, she'd known that she'd had to try it on. It had fitted perfectly so she'd taken a deep breath then told the assistant that she would buy it. It had made a big hole in her savings but, as she studied her reflection, Emma knew that it had been worth every penny.

It was a classic shift style that made the most of her slender curves. From the front it appeared almost staid, with its high neckline and rather severe lines. However, it was an entirely different story from the back!

Emma smiled as she twisted round so that she could see the lace insert which dipped in a V shape almost to her waist. There was no doubt that the dress was guaranteed to attract a second or even a third glance! Ridiculously high-heeled, black suede sandals—another impulsive buy in the sales—completed the picture of sophistication. All in all, she didn't think that Daniel would be too disappointed.

The sound of the doorbell made her jump. Emma pressed her hand to her racing heart as she made her way downstairs to let Daniel in.

'You look wonderful, Emma.' His hazel eyes swept over her with such undisguised appreciation that she laughed.

'So do you. Very handsome and distinguished, in fact.'

She was pleased to hear that her voice sounded light, though she meant every word. Daniel was wearing a well-cut dinner suit with a snowy white shirt and black bow-tie, and he looked absolutely stunning.

'Reckon it beats the white coat, do you?' he asked with a grin.

'Just!' Emma laughed when he glowered at her. 'Don't go fishing for compliments then you won't be disappointed.'

'Would I do such a thing? *Moi?*' he declared, in all innocence.

'Yes! Anyway, I'll just fetch my coat, otherwise we'll be late.' Emma ran back upstairs to fetch her coat and bag. Daniel had the door open when she came back down. He cast an assessing look at the snowy pavement then an equally assessing one at her feet in the strappy sandals.

'Well, in the absence of a cloak…' He swept her up into

his arms, grinning when he saw the surprise on her face. 'You'll get frostbite, going out into the snow in those shoes, Emma.'

He dropped a kiss on the tip of her nose then stepped out of the door. 'Hang on tight! And no wriggling. I don't want to drop you!'

'Oh, my hero!' Emma teased, hanging on for dear life as he slid and slipped his way to his car. He managed to open the door and deposited her on the passenger seat. 'Who says the age of chivalry is dead?'

'Anyone who doesn't want a hernia!' Daniel retorted with a wicked grin. He ducked when she reached for a handful of snow. 'Only joking—honest! You're as light as a feather.'

He slammed the door then made a great performance of clutching his back as he walked round to the driver's side. He stamped the snow off his feet before he got in, grinning at her as she rolled her eyes. 'I can see you aren't impressed by my acting so I may as well give it up as a bad job. Let's get going. This is going to be a night to remember, and we don't want to waste a minute of it!'

And it was a night to remember. From the moment they arrived, Daniel went out of his way to make sure that Emma was having a good time. Emma knew that they were the object of many curious pairs of eyes as they danced the night away, but she didn't care what people were thinking.

Mike Humphreys was there, partnered by a new nurse from A and E. He glowered at Emma as she and Daniel danced past but even that didn't spoil her enjoyment. Just being with Daniel, that made the whole evening special. She felt as though nothing could spoil it for her.

There was a buffet supper served at ten o'clock and they joined the queue waiting to be served. Outside caterers had been hired for the occasion and the food was delicious— smoked salmon, ham, beef, turkey and wonderful salads.

Linda and Gary were just ahead of them, waiting to be served, and Linda groaned when she saw the magnificent spread.

'Oh, bang goes my diet! I'm going to look like a meringue, walking down that aisle, if I'm not careful!' She gave Emma a cheeky smile. 'Not something you'll need to worry about on your wedding day, Em.'

Linda shot a pointed look at Daniel and Emma flushed. She could cheerfully have throttled her friend for saying that. She had no idea what Daniel must be thinking so hurried to limit any damage that might have been caused.

'I'm not planning on getting married for a long time to come, so you can stop throwing out hints, Linda. Just because you're eager to tie yourself down doesn't mean that we're all like you!'

Linda laughed good-naturedly as she took her turn at the buffet table. Emma shot an anxious look at Daniel but he wasn't looking at her. He was staring into the distance and there was an expression of such pain on his face that her heart ached.

'Is anything wrong?' she asked him softly, driven to ask.

He shook his head and it seemed as though a mask had fallen over his face all of a sudden. 'Of course not. What could be wrong?'

He smiled but there was no real warmth in it. Emma shivered, though she couldn't have explained why she felt chilled all of a sudden. It was their turn to select from the buffet so she didn't say anything else. However, the episode seemed to cast a shadow over the evening. Nothing was quite the same after that, although Daniel was as attentive as he had been earlier. When he suggested that they leave just before midnight, Emma agreed at once.

He drove her home without saying very much. He seemed to have a lot on his mind and Emma didn't know how to start up a conversation. When they stopped outside her flat, she noticed that he didn't switch off the engine.

'Would you like to come in for coffee?' she invited, hoping that he would accept. Maybe it was silly but she *knew* that something was wrong. Perhaps she could get him to talk about it over coffee.

'I won't, thanks. You've had a busy day and I'm sure you must want to get to bed.' He kissed her cheek but the kiss was so impersonal that Emma felt her eyes mist with tears. It was like one of those social kisses strangers bestowed on one another, completely devoid of meaning.

It was an effort to behave as though nothing was wrong. 'I'll bring Amy's presents round to your house tomorrow so that you can wrap them. What time would suit you best?'

'I have the afternoon off as it's Christmas Eve. Would two o'clock suit you? Say if it isn't convenient.'

How polite he sounded! They could have been two strangers for all the emotion he showed. Emma couldn't bear it any longer and reached for the handle.

'Fine. Two o'clock it is, then.'

She heard the taut note in her voice and knew Daniel must have heard it, too, because his hands tightened on the steering-wheel, although he didn't say anything else.

Emma got out of the car and carefully picked her way across the pavement, thinking back to what had happened earlier when Daniel had carried her to his car. What had gone wrong? Why was he so distant all of a sudden?

Daniel waited only long enough to see her safely inside before he drove away.

Emma went straight up to her flat and into her bedroom. Her sandals were probably ruined from their soaking in the snow but she didn't care. She stood in front of the mirror, thinking back to how she'd felt a few hours earlier. All the excitement had gone and all the anticipation along with it. What a fool she'd been to hope for more than she could ever have. What a fool to hope that Daniel might ever come to care for her!

CHAPTER ELEVEN

IT WAS almost one a.m. when Emma was woken by the sound of someone ringing her doorbell. Tossing back the bedclothes, she hurried to the window and peered down into the street but she couldn't see who it was. She was tempted not to answer but the thought of the people in the other flats being woken made her decide that she couldn't ignore it.

Fastening her dressing-gown around her, she ran downstairs and was shocked to find Mike Humphreys standing on the step. It was obvious from the way he was swaying that he was very drunk.

'Ah, Emma…pretty, scheming, little Emma,' he slurred, lurching towards her.

Emma pushed him away, feeling her stomach heave when she caught the smell of alcohol on his breath. 'What do you want, Mike? Have you any idea what time it is?'

He peered blearily at his watch then shook his head. 'Nope! Still, it's not that late, is it? Aren't you going to invite me in for a cup of coffee, Em, seeing as I've come all this way to see you?'

Before she could stop him, he'd stepped inside and closed the door. He leered as he noticed her dressing-gown. 'Oops, did I wake you up? I hope I didn't wake his lordship as well. That will have really blotted my copybook, won't it? Mind you, it's so full of blots now that I don't suppose it will make much difference.'

He laughed loudly at his own joke. Emma shook his arm as she saw a light come on in the ground-floor flat. 'Shh! You'll wake everyone up. Look, Mike, you're drunk so the best thing you can do is to get yourself off home.'

'So I don't interrupt your little party?' He shook his head so hard that he staggered against the wall. 'No, now I'm here I'm staying. It wouldn't be sociable if I didn't pay my respects to my revered boss.'

'Daniel isn't here if that's what you think,' Emma told him shortly. She shook her head when Mike opened his mouth. 'I mean it, Mike. Now, come along. It's time you went home.'

She steered him to the door but he resisted her efforts to usher him out. 'So Hutton didn't get any further with you than the rest of us have? Oh, dear, he wouldn't have liked that.'

Emma felt sick as she realised what he meant. 'My relationship with Daniel—or anyone else for that matter—is none of your business. Now, I want you to leave.'

She pushed him out of the door then paused when she saw his car parked in the road. 'You didn't drive here!' she exclaimed in horror.

Mike shrugged then had to grab hold of the wall to stop himself falling over. 'Course. Why not?'

'Because you're drunk, that's why!' Emma held out her hand. 'Give me the car keys—now!'

He took a bit of persuading before he finally handed them over. Emma shoved them in her pocket then realised that now she was faced with the problem of how he would get home. Finding a taxi at this hour could be difficult. Clearsea didn't boast much in the way of nightlife so there were few taxis running after midnight.

She sighed as she realised that she had no choice but to drive Mike home herself. She certainly couldn't take the risk of him wandering about on such a cold night in that state.

'Stay there.'

She ran back to her flat and dragged on jeans and a sweater. Mike was sitting on the step when she arrived back downstairs. He had his eyes closed and was snoring loudly as the effects of the alcohol caught up with him. It was a struggle to wake him and get him into the car. Emma muttered under her breath as she started the engine. The last thing she felt like doing was driving across town at this time of the night!

It was almost two before she arrived back home. Mike's flatmate had taken some rousing but she'd finally been able to hand over the young houseman into someone else's care. She switched off the engine then gasped as the car door was wrenched open.

'Where the hell have you been?'

Emma blinked, not quite able to believe that her eyes weren't deceiving her. What on earth was Daniel doing here?

'I...um...I went to Mike's. He—'

Daniel didn't let her finish. 'Forget it. I don't want to know what you've been up to because it isn't any of my business. Hurry up. I've wasted enough time waiting around here as it is.'

He turned and strode to his car. He had the engine running before she'd even got out of hers. Emma ran over to the car but Daniel didn't even look at her.

'Get in.'

'Why? What's happening? Look, Daniel, what is this?'

'Amy's been hurt. She's in hospital and she's asking for you.' He looked at her then and his eyes were as hard as pebbles. 'That's the only reason I'm here, because Amy wants you.'

Emma got into the car without another word. She could feel her heart hammering with fear. There was also a burning pain in her chest but she didn't allow herself to think about it. It was Amy who mattered now, not what Daniel thought about her. Just Amy. For now...

'The good news is that the scan is clear. There is no obvious damage to Amy's skull.'

'But there could be bruising to the brain, couldn't there?'

Daniel was as taut as a coiled spring. Emma ached to comfort him, only she knew that he wouldn't thank her for her concern. He'd briefly explained what had happened on the drive to the hospital. Evidently, Amy and the rest of the children at the sleep-over party had crept out of bed while her friend's parents were asleep and had gone into the garden to play with snowballs.

Unfortunately, Amy had slipped on a patch of ice and had hit her head on the edge of the patio. Daniel had arrived back from the dance to find a message on his answering machine, telling him that Amy had been taken to hospital. Emma knew that he must be tormenting himself with the thought that he should have been there and that it had added to his distress.

'I'm not going to lie and say that it isn't a possibility.' Lee Brennan, the young Casualty doctor on duty that night, shrugged. He was doing his pre-registration training and it was obvious that he was a little in awe of Daniel so was being very careful about what he said.

'You know enough about head injuries, sir, to understand that it's always a concern. However, we're hopeful that Amy has suffered nothing more serious than concussion, so let's try to be positive.'

Lee turned to Emma with relief when Daniel didn't say anything. 'Amy has been asking for you, Emma, so why don't you go and see her? We want to keep her as quiet as possible for the next twenty-four hours.'

'Of course.' Emma didn't look at Daniel as she hurriedly made her way to the side room where Amy had been taken. The little girl had her eyes closed, a huge bruise on her right temple telling its own tale about her exploits that night.

Emma felt a lump come to her throat as she looked at the small figure in the bed. She had grown to love Amy as though she were her own and it hurt to see her lying there, looking so ill.

'Emma...you came. Uncle Daniel promised that you would...'

Emma sat down by the bed and took hold of the little girl's hand as Amy opened her eyes. 'Of course I came. What was that I heard about you cracking a flagstone with your head?' she teased, earning herself a wan smile.

'I slid over in the snow and it hurt.' The little girl raised her hand to her head but Emma gently stopped her. Amy was attached to a drip and she didn't want her pulling out the IV line.

'I know. You've got a wonderful bruise on your forehead. It's every colour of the rainbow.'

Amy smiled. 'Is it? Can I see?'

'Maybe later. You just lie there nice and still and it will make you feel better.' Emma looked round as Daniel came to join her. He barely glanced at her, however, as he drew up a chair to the other side of his niece's bed.

'Hi, horror. How do you feel now?'

Amy smiled. 'Better 'cos Emma's here.'

Daniel glanced across the bed and for a moment his expression was unguarded. Emma inwardly recoiled when she saw the pain in his eyes. Surely she wasn't responsible for putting it there?

It was impossible to tell, of course. However, when Daniel turned away she heard the rough note in his voice and knew in her heart that she was right.

'Emma cares a lot about you, poppet. That's why she came. Now, you be a good girl and rest then you'll soon be better.'

'Will you stay...both of you?' Amy clutched tightly to their two hands.

Daniel looked at Emma and she nodded, although she couldn't help wondering why he'd needed to ask. Surely he must know that she would stay with Amy for however long the little girl needed her there?

She sighed. Maybe not. It seemed there was a lot that Daniel didn't know about her.

It was a long night. Amy became increasingly fretful because she was tired. Emma knew that the child couldn't understand why the nurses kept waking her. However, it was imperative that they checked for any deterioration in her condition. By the time morning came, all three of them were worn out.

Daniel stood up and stretched as a different nurse came in with a drink for the little girl. His face was grey with fatigue, contrasting with the white of his evening shirt. He must have rushed straight to the hospital as soon as he'd heard the message, and Emma couldn't help thinking how awful it must have been for him.

He beckoned her over to the window as the nurse ran through the obs once more. 'There's no point in you staying any longer, Emma. Why don't you go home? You can come back later if you want to.'

It was said so indifferently that Emma had to bite back a retort. Daniel was tired and worried so it was neither the time nor the place to make a fuss, though it hurt to have him speak to her that way.

'I'd rather stay,' she said flatly. 'I don't want Amy getting upset because I'm not here.'

'Fine. That's up to you, of course.'

He went back to the bed, smiling as he bent to speak to his niece. Emma felt herself choke up with emotion because it was obvious that Daniel was deliberately trying to cut her out. She couldn't understand why he was behaving that way but there was little she could do about it. She certainly wouldn't risk upsetting Amy by causing an argument! However, when the duty doctor arrived to check on the little girl, she took the opportunity to slip away to the canteen for a cup of coffee. The atmosphere in the room was so oppressive that she simply had to take a break.

There were few people about at that time of the morning. Emma paid for her drink and also bought a croissant, though she really didn't feel hungry. She had just sat down when Mike Humphreys appeared at her table.

He held up his hands placatingly. 'I know what you're going to say, Em, and you're well within your rights. I behaved abominably.'

'Well, you said it.' Emma picked up her cup, wishing that he would go away. She certainly didn't want to speak to him after what had happened the previous night. However, he pulled out a chair and sat down.

'I'm not going to make excuses because there aren't any. I just want to say thanks for what you did last night by driving me home.' He ran his hand over his face and sighed. 'I can't believe that I was actually going to drive in the state I was in.'

'It was stupid.' Emma had no intention of letting him off the hook. 'You could have killed yourself or, worse still, you could have killed somebody else.'

'I know, I know. I've been acting like a complete idiot of late. I just wanted you to know that I'm sorry, both about last night and everything else.'

'What do you mean?'

Mike shifted uncomfortably. 'It was me who started those rumours about Paula Walters's ring, Em. I was peeved because you'd made it obvious that you weren't interested in me.' He laughed hollowly. 'The old ego got the better of me, I'm afraid.'

Emma stood up because she didn't want to spend another second in his company. 'That was a horrible thing to do, Mike! Now, if you'll excuse me, I'm needed elsewhere.'

'I heard about Hutton's niece. How's she doing?' Mike grimaced when he saw her sceptical expression. 'Look, I don't wish any harm to come to the kid.'

'She's fine.' She turned away, leaving most of her coffee and all the croissant untouched.

'You really are keen on Hutton, aren't you? I hope he appreciates how lucky he is.'

Emma didn't pause as she hurriedly left the canteen. There was a bitter pain in her chest as she thought about what Mike had said. She doubted very much if Daniel would appreciate how she felt about him after the way he'd been behaving in the past few hours!

Amy was asleep when she got back to the room and Daniel was slumped in a chair. Emma thought at first that he was asleep as well but he suddenly looked up.

'The doctors are hopeful that she'll be allowed home later today,' he announced flatly.

'That's good. At least she'll still be able to enjoy her Christmas.'

Daniel smiled thinly. 'Yes, that's another thing to be grateful for. At least all your hard work won't have been in vain, Emma.'

There was a certain harshness in his voice, though he'd spoken quietly so as not to disturb the sleeping child. Emma frowned.

'What do you mean by that, Daniel?'

'Nothing. Forget it.' He stood up, motioning Emma to follow him from the room. His tone was devoid of expression as he continued.

'I'm going to be tied up here most of the day so I was wondering if you would mind wrapping up Amy's presents and getting things ready for tomorrow. I take it that you still intend to carry on as we arranged?'

'Of course.' She didn't ask him why he thought that she might have changed her mind. It was obvious that Daniel was deliberately trying to put their arrangements on a solely businesslike footing so she wasn't going to make the mistake of letting personal feelings creep in. However, that didn't mean she wasn't hurt by his attitude or that she understood it.

Last night at the dance had been so wonderful. Then there had been that night she'd stayed at his house. That had been even more wonderful! Yet it was hard to believe that she'd shared either experience with this man who now spoke to her so coldly.

'Then I can safely leave everything to you, Emma. Thank you.'

He turned and went back into his niece's room without a backward glance. Emma took a deep breath. She wouldn't make a fool of herself by breaking down. That would be unforgivable. She would carry on as they'd planned—make sure that Amy had the most wonderful Christmas Day. Then she would slip quietly out of Daniel's life...

That was it! Everything was wrapped.

Emma sighed in relief as she studied the mound of gaily wrapped parcels stacked on the end of Daniel's bed. She'd decided to wrap Amy's presents in his bedroom in case he brought his niece home earlier than expected. He'd rung to say that they should be home by four but Emma knew enough about hospitals not to take that for granted.

Now she picked up two of the presents and took them downstairs to the sitting room where she placed them under the Christmas tree. There were a few other parcels there already and she smiled when she recognised one as being Amy's present to her uncle. What *would* Daniel make of that tie?

Her smile faded when it struck her that she wouldn't be around to know if he wore it very often. Once Christmas Day was over Daniel and his niece wouldn't need her in their lives any longer. What they did wouldn't be any of her concern, and although it was bitterly painful to know that, it would be foolish not to face the facts.

The sound of a car drawing up warned her that Daniel

and Amy were arriving. Emma fixed a smile to her face as she went to greet them.

'Hello, there! How do you feel, Amy? Is your head still sore?'

'A bit, but the doctor said I could come home. I was glad 'cos I was worried in case Father Christmas didn't know where to find me,' Amy explained seriously.

'Oh, I'm sure Santa would have found out where you were,' Emma assured her. 'He always manages to deliver presents to the boys and girls who have to stay in hospital over Christmas.'

'He must be really clever, mustn't he?' Amy said, obviously impressed.

'Oh, he is!' Emma took the little girl's coat and led her into the sitting room. She was very aware that Daniel hadn't said a word since he'd entered the house. She shot him a wary glance but he avoided her eyes as he made his niece comfortable on the sofa.

'Now, remember what the doctor told you, Amy? That you have to be a good girl and rest.' He smiled at the child. 'Then you'll be well enough to enjoy yourself tomorrow. OK?'

'OK.' Amy agreed obediently.

She looked worn out, poor little mite, Emma thought, seeing the shadows under the little girl's eyes. She felt suddenly sick with relief that Amy hadn't suffered any worse injuries. She knew how dangerous knocks to the head could be…

'Emma?'

She looked up with a start when she realised that Daniel was speaking to her. 'Yes?'

'I just asked if you wanted a cup of tea,' he said politely.

'I'll make it,' Emma offered immediately, conscious of the way he was looking so intently at her.

She hurried from the room and went into the kitchen to fill the kettle. She didn't realise at first that he'd followed her, and jumped when she turned and saw him standing by the table.

'Are you all right?' he asked flatly.

'Of course. Why shouldn't I be?' she snapped back, stung into replying that way by the indifference in his voice. Did he have any idea how it hurt to have him speak to her like that? Probably not! Why should Daniel care about her feelings?

'Because you're acting so strangely, of course. You were miles away just now. You had no idea I was speaking to you.'

He paused and his tone was clipped all of a sudden. 'Maybe you were wishing that you didn't have to waste time here when you could be spending it with someone who's really important to you. Well, don't let us keep you, Emma. Amy and I can manage perfectly well without you!'

'Fine! If that's how you feel, I may as well leave.' Emma hurried towards the door. She was so hurt that he could say such a thing that all she wanted to do was leave before she broke down. Tears filled her eyes and she let out a gasp of pain as she walked into the end of the table and banged her hip.

'Careful!'

Daniel was beside her in an instant. He swore softly when he saw the tears running down her face. 'You've hurt yourself. Here, sit down…'

'No!' Emma pushed him away when he tried to guide her to a chair. 'I'm fine. Don't waste time worrying about me, Daniel. I know you don't want me here so I'll leave.'

'What do you mean—*I* don't want you here? It's you who wants to be somewhere else. I can hazard a guess as to where as well. Tell Humphreys that I'm sorry for taking up so much of your time of late but that it won't happen again!'

He pointedly stepped aside but Emma didn't move. 'I don't know how many times I need to repeat this before it sinks in,' she bit out through clenched teeth, 'but Mike Humphreys hasn't any claim on my time!'

'Oh, no? Look, Emma, it isn't my business, so—'

She didn't let him finish because she was sick and tired of hearing him speak to her in that…that *know-it-all* tone! 'You're right, Daniel. It isn't any of your business. You've made it clear that you don't want it to be *your* business! However, for your information, there never has been, nor will there ever be, anything going on between Mike and me. Got the message now?'

She started to walk past him but his hand fastened around her wrist and drew her to a halt. Emma felt her breath catch because there was an expression on his face that she'd never seen there before. Why did Daniel look so…so scared all of a sudden? She had no idea but it certainly scared her!

'Do you really mean that, Emma? I know you've told me before that you and Humphreys weren't involved, but last night…' He broke off.

Emma could see the struggle he was having but there was nothing she could do to help him. It would be wrong to read more into what was happening than Daniel might mean, even though her foolish heart was already writing whole chapters about it!

'What happened last night, Emma? I must have phoned you a dozen times from the hospital. I was so worried when I couldn't get an answer that I went to your flat to see if you were all right. I was ready to rouse everyone in the whole house after I rang your bell and didn't get a reply. Then, lo and behold, you appeared and told me that you'd been with Humphreys. What was I to think?'

'I've no idea. Maybe you should have given me chance to tell you that when Mike turned up drunk at my door I confiscated his car keys. Then I could have explained that it meant I'd had to drive him home myself. That's what happened, you see, Daniel. Not very exciting, was it?'

'Oh, Emma, I'm sorry! I'm such an idiot, aren't I? If only I'd given you chance to explain!'

'Uh-huh.' She gave him a tight little smile. 'You are an idiot, Daniel!'

He chuckled. 'I can see that you aren't going to let me off too lightly. I don't blame you. I did rather jump to conclusions. I was so keyed up with everything that had happened that I wasn't thinking rationally. Will you forgive me?'

How could she refuse when she heard the entreaty in his voice? 'There's nothing to forgive. It was a misunderstanding. So long as you accept that I'm not interested in Mike, and certainly not after what he told me this morning.'

'What do you mean?'

Emma quickly explained about Mike having started the rumours, and she saw Daniel's face darken. 'I bet it was Humphreys who contacted the police as well. I wondered who was responsible for that.'

'Probably.' Emma shrugged. 'I didn't ask him. I was so sickened by what he told me that I didn't want to hear any more.'

'Why did he do it, though?' Daniel frowned. 'If he was keen on you, it was a funny way of showing how he felt.'

'I think he was trying to get back at me for refusing to go out with him,' Emma explained.

'Also, he was probably annoyed because I was taking up so much of your time. Humphreys and I haven't seen eye to eye since I started working at St Luke's. I don't like his attitude and he knows it.' Daniel sighed. 'I seem to have caused you a lot of problems, Emma. I bet you're sorry you ever agreed to help me.'

'That's where you're wrong. I've enjoyed every minute. I'm only sorry that once Christmas is over it will have to end.' She hadn't meant to say that and wished she could take it back when she saw him look sharply at her.

'Because you'll miss being with Amy?' Daniel's voice

was flat. 'I know that you've grown fond of her, Emma, and I know how fond she is of you. However, it wouldn't be fair to expect you to give up any more of your time, nor would it be fair to Amy to let her grow even more attached to you. I know you aren't interested in that kind of commitment.'

'Why do you think that?' she asked quietly, although her heart was thumping so hard that it was difficult to think straight.

'Because of what you told Linda last night. You were quite honest about not wanting to get tied down just yet, and who can blame you?'

'I know what I told Linda. I know why I said it as well.' Emma coloured. 'Linda was throwing out hints about you and me, and I didn't want her embarrassing you.'

'But you must have meant it, surely?'

She heard the uncertainty in his voice and her hands clenched. Why did she have a feeling that her answer was important to him? 'Not really. I'm certainly not trying to avoid commitment, if that's what you thought.'

'I see.' He turned away, picked up the kettle then put it down again with a thud. Emma saw his shoulders rise and fall as he took a deep breath before he suddenly swung round to face her once more.

'I swore that I wouldn't say this but what you've just told me has changed everything. Having you in my life these past weeks has been the best thing that has ever happened to me, Emma. I go cold thinking about what it's going to be like when I can no longer use Christmas as an excuse to be with you.

'I promised myself that I would *never* use Amy as an inducement, but I can't help myself. I know that you enjoy being with her. I know that you would agree to continue being part of our lives for her benefit. I'm desperate enough to use all of those to my own ends, though it doesn't make me feel proud of myself for doing so.'

Emma's head was swimming. She could barely take in what he was saying. 'Wh-why are you so desperate to have me in your life, Daniel? I don't understand.'

'Because I'm head over heels in love with you, of course! Surely it's obvious?'

He sounded so amazed that Emma laughed out loud. 'Not at all. I can honestly say that I had no idea how you felt about me!'

Maybe he sensed something from her tone because his expression suddenly lightened. 'Well, if it's a surprise then I have to say that you're taking it extremely well. You don't look as though you're about to turn tail and run.'

'Don't I?' She smiled as he came and stood in front of her, and wondered how she could tease him at such a momentous time in her life.

'No. In fact, if I were a betting man I'd say that there was a greater than even chance that the idea never crossed your mind.' His smile was slow and sexy, a growing confidence creeping back into his voice.

'You could be right. Of course, you really need to study form before you place a bet.' Emma was enjoying herself now. There was something deliciously enticing about drawing out the moment when she would tell him how she felt.

'Oh, I'm fairly confident that I'm on a winner.'

'So you don't want to know what odds I'm offering?'

'Well, I suppose it can't hurt.' He smiled at her. 'So, what are the odds on you not running out of here?'

'Oh, a hundred to zero against…'

Emma didn't manage to finish. Daniel obviously had other things on his mind by that point! He swept her into his arms and kissed her so thoroughly that Emma wasn't capable of standing upright let alone running.

His eyes were full of wonder as he gazed at her. 'I can't believe this. You are sure, Emma? I mean, you're sure how you feel about me and it isn't just that you love Amy…?'

'Shh.' She pressed her fingers against his lips. 'I know how I feel, Daniel Hutton. I love you.'

He closed his eyes and she felt him take a huge breath. 'Thank heavens for that! I've been dreading this Christmas as much as I've been looking forward to it.' He opened his eyes and looked at her with a wealth of love. 'Now I know that Christmas is the beginning, not the end as I feared it would be.'

Emma smiled as she reached up and kissed him. 'I think that's very appropriate, don't you? Christmas should be a time when wonderful things start to happen.'

Daniel smiled back at her. 'You're right. I love you, Emma Graham. I wish I could show you how much only there's a small girl in the sitting room who's bound to be wondering where we've got to—'

He broke off when, on cue, there was a shout from the other room of, 'Uncle Daniel, Emma, where are you?'

Emma laughed as she slid out of his arms. 'It appears that we're wanted. I think we shall have to leave the demonstrations for now, don't you?'

CHAPTER TWELVE

IT WAS well past nine before Amy settled down to sleep. Daniel came downstairs after tucking her up in bed and flopped down onto the sofa.

'Thanks heavens for that! I thought she would *never* give in.'

Emma laughed as she snuggled against him. 'She's so excited, isn't she? Did you see her face when we were arranging the glass of sherry and mince pie for Santa?'

'I did.' Daniel laughed softly as he looked at the mantelpiece which now bore Amy's offerings. 'Isn't it lovely when a child believes so fervently that there's a Father Christmas?'

'You mean there isn't one?' Emma feigned surprise. Daniel laughed as he pulled her closer and kissed her lingeringly.

'Let's just say that I'm beginning to have second thoughts on the subject,' he replied rather thickly several, highly satisfying minutes later. 'A couple of weeks ago I would have stated categorically that Santa didn't exist but after what's happened recently I'm not so sure. There has to be some explanation for why I've received such a wonderful gift.'

'And what gift would that be?' Emma asked smugly, already sure what the answer would be.

'You. As if you needed to be told!' Daniel kissed her again in loving punishment for her temerity. 'Knowing that you're going to be a permanent fixture in my life is the best present I could have hoped for, Emma. Have I told you how much I love you, by the way?'

'I think you did mention it but that was *hours* ago. It

wouldn't hurt to tell me again because I certainly won't get tired of hearing you say it.'

'Good.' He took her face between his hands. 'I love you, Emma. You have made my life complete, though I had no idea there was anything missing from it before you came along.'

She laughed a little shakily because she was so touched by the depth of emotion in his voice. 'So you thought that you had everything you wanted before my advent into your life, did you?'

'I did.' He sighed softly as he pulled her back into his arms and held her close. 'I had my job and I had Amy—that seemed enough. Oh, I've had relationships in the past but they were just temporary affairs in all senses. I'd never met anyone I wanted to spend my life with.'

'Me, too. Or is it me neither? Whichever. What I mean is that I'd never met anyone I wanted to share my life with before I met you, Daniel.'

'I'm glad. It makes what we have all the more special, doesn't it? As though we each have been waiting for the other to come along.'

'It does. And we have Amy to thank for it happening. If you hadn't been desperate enough to ask me if I could sew, we might never have got together,' she said wonderingly.

'Oh, I don't know about that.' Daniel's tone was so wry that she shifted slightly so that she could look at him. He kissed the tip of her nose then grinned. 'I was very much aware of you, Staff Nurse Graham. You had impinged on my consciousness in a big way.'

'I had? But you never said anything…' She took a deep breath. 'You never *showed* how you felt either!'

'Mmm, discretion being the better part of valour and all that.' He laughed deeply. 'I'd heard that you were very choosy about who you dated and I was scared of getting turned down. It wouldn't have done much for my ego, I can tell you!'

He sobered. 'Also, I was very much aware that my first duty was to Amy. I didn't have the time for a relationship and couldn't imagine any woman wanting to get herself lumbered with looking after someone else's child.

'I'd been dating someone when Claire died and she made it clear that she didn't intend being a surrogate mother to Amy. Not that there was *any* chance of me asking her to be, I might add. However, it did bring it home to me that most women would take a very dim view of taking responsibility for someone else's child.'

It explained a lot, Emma thought. She hurried to reassure him. 'I'm not them, though, Daniel. I love Amy. I can't think of anything I want more than to be able to play a part in bringing her up, if you'll let me.'

'I can't imagine doing it alone now. I've seen how Amy has blossomed under your care, Emma. She needs you as much as she needs me. Together we shall be able to give her all the love and stability that Claire would have given her.'

Emma felt humbled to hear him say that. She kissed him quickly. 'We shall. We'll try our best to be good parents to her, Daniel.'

'And to our own children as well.'

Emma heard the question in his voice and smiled at him. 'And for them as well.'

It seemed pointless wasting time on words at that point. Emma wasn't sure how much time had passed when Daniel finally raised his head. She loved him so much that the world seemed to stop when she was in his arms! However, a glance at the clock on the mantelpiece showed her how late it was and she reluctantly stood up.

'Much as I hate to break up the party, it's time I left.'

'You're going home? But I thought you'd stay the night here?' Daniel's voice betrayed how he felt about the idea of her leaving.

'I don't want to leave but I was worried about what Amy

might think if I stay here again—' she began, but he cut her off.

'We shall explain the situation to Amy in the morning if she asks,' he stated firmly. 'Once she knows we're getting married she'll understand.'

'Married?' Emma gulped. She saw Daniel smile as he stood up and took hold of her hands.

'Uh-huh. You will marry me, won't you, Emma? I know it's an old-fashioned idea in today's world but it's what I want more than anything.'

'Then I suppose I must be an old-fashioned sort of woman because it's what I want, too. Yes, Daniel, I will marry you.'

'Great!' He swung her off her feet and twirled her round.

'Has Father Christmas been?' a hopeful little voice demanded from the doorway.

Daniel chuckled as he set Emma back on her feet and turned to his niece. 'Not yet, sweetheart. But I'm sure he's on his way.'

'Oh! Then why were you and Emma so excited?' Amy asked, looking sleepily from Emma to her uncle.

'Because Emma and I are getting married.' He picked up the little girl and kissed her. 'Which means that Emma is going to be living here with us soon. Won't that be nice?'

'Mmm.' Amy smiled her delight then suddenly frowned. 'You'll have to make sure that Father Christmas knows that you're going to live with us, Emma, or he might not be able to bring you your presents.'

Emma laughed as she kissed the child's cheek. 'I'll do that! Now it's time you went back to bed. Father Christmas won't bring your presents unless you're fast asleep.'

'Will you take me?' Amy asked.

Emma lifted the little girl out of Daniel's arms and hugged her. 'Of course I will.'

She looked at Daniel over the top of Amy's head as she carried her from the room. She could see in his eyes everything that she was feeling. They would share their lives and their love with this precious child and become a family. It seemed her wish had come true after all.

Christmas Day passed in a whirl from the moment they were woken by Amy's excited cries when she discovered her presents. Both Emma and Daniel went into the little girl's room and watched her unwrap them.

Amy was thrilled with everything, particularly the doll and the pot-bellied pig puzzle. Emma's help was enlisted as she tipped the pieces of puzzle onto the floor.

That took a couple of hours, although Amy did break off several times to play with the doll and draw some pictures with her new crayons. Daniel made them all tea and toast then it was time to unwrap the presents under the tree.

Amy loved her sweater and insisted on wearing it right away. Emma helped her put it on then watched as the child solemnly presented Daniel with his present.

'It's wonderful,' he declared, immediately putting the tie round his neck and knotting it under the collar of his dressing-gown. 'It's the best tie I've ever had!'

'I knew you'd like it,' she said happily, then dug through the parcels and produced one for Emma. 'Uncle Daniel helped me choose this. He said that you'd like it.'

Emma unwrapped the many layers of paper and was touched to find a bottle of her favourite perfume inside. 'It's my favourite! How did you know?'

'Oh, it took a lot of sniffing and testing before we tracked it down, didn't it, Amy?' Daniel winked at his niece. 'I think the lady in the shop was glad when we finally decided which one it was!'

'I can imagine!' Emma laughed as she handed him the present she'd bought for him. 'I hope you like this.'

'It's beautiful!' Daniel placed the glass paperweight in pride of place on the mantelpiece. 'I could even use those colours when I decorate in here.'

Emma and Amy exchanged horrified looks. 'I think we prefer *beige* to shocking pink, don't we, Amy?'

Daniel laughed. 'Spoilsports! Anyway, now it's your turn to see what I bought for you. I hope you like it, too, Emma.'

He handed her a small package wrapped in gold paper. Emma frowned as she worked the sticky tape away from one end. She had no idea at all what it could be. She gasped when she opened the velvet box and discovered a beautiful gold locket inside.

'It's gorgeous, Daniel. I don't know what to say.'

'I'm glad you like it. Look inside.'

Emma carefully unfastened the tiny clasp and opened the locket to reveal photographs of Daniel and Amy. She was so touched that she couldn't say a word because she knew in her heart what it symbolised. Daniel was giving her himself and Amy as her Christmas present, and she knew that she could never have been given anything more wonderful or more special than that.

'I came downstairs and put the pictures in it while you were asleep last night,' he explained, drawing her aside as Amy started playing with some of her new toys. 'The locket was my mother's and I had the jeweller fit a new chain because the old one was broken. I was going to give it to you empty, but after last night I realised that the locket was just a token and that the gift I really wanted you to accept was Amy and me.'

He drew her round to face him. 'I know I've asked you this before, but will you marry me, Emma?'

'And I've told you before but I don't mind saying it again—yes, I'll marry you, Daniel. There couldn't be a better, more wonderful gift than the one you've given me.'

Emma knew he understood that she didn't mean just the locket. He kissed her gently then looked up when Amy sighed heavily.

'I suppose this means that you two will be kissing and stuff all the time, doesn't it?'

'Very possibly,' Daniel replied, completely deadpan. 'Why? Is it a problem, Amy?'

'S'pose not. But I'm never going to kiss a boy. It's really yucky!'

Emma laughed. 'We'll remind her of that in a few years' time, shall we?' she asked softly as Amy went back to her toys.

'Don't! Can you imagine what it's going to be like when boyfriends appear on the horizon?' Daniel's expression was horrified.

'We'll cope,' Emma assured him. 'We'll be fully qualified parents by that stage.'

'I'll remind you of that when the time comes,' he growled, obviously not convinced.

Emma just laughed then suddenly caught sight of the time. 'Look at the time! Why didn't you say something?'

'Say what? What's wrong?' Daniel demanded in alarm.

'What's wrong is that I have a turkey to get in the oven and it had better be soon otherwise we'll be eating Christmas dinner at midnight!'

She rushed out of the room, smiling when she heard Daniel laugh. She set to work in the kitchen and he joined her a short time later, helping her peel the vegetables and get everything ready. It was obvious that he wanted it to be special as well, and it would be. It was going to be their first Christmas dinner together, the first of many to come!

'So I opened this cracker and there was a ring. Gary had been back to the jeweller's and bought it for me because he knew how disappointed I was.'

Linda held out her hand so that they could all admire the dainty diamond solitaire she was sporting. It was their first day back after the Christmas break and they were all gathered in the staffroom, getting ready to go on duty and swopping stories about what they had done.

'It's beautiful, Linda. Wasn't that a lovely thing for Gary to do?' Emma said.

'It was. He can be quite thoughtful at times.' Linda smiled. 'Then he can be a real pain at others! Still, he's my pain and I love him.'

'Oh, she's getting soft in her old age,' Eileen Pierce remarked with a laugh.

'Not at all,' Linda denied swiftly. 'It's just an overload of Christmas spirit. Anyway, how was your Christmas, Em? Did you enjoy it as much as you thought you would?'

'It was even better than I'd hoped,' Emma replied dreamily. She coloured when she heard the others chuckle but there was no way she could keep what had happened a secret. She was dying to tell everyone her news.

'Daniel and I are getting married.'

'What! You are? Why, you dark horse, you! Mind, I knew there was something afoot. I could smell it in the air!'

Linda hugged her hard as the others offered their congratulations. Emma laughed.

'I still can't believe it. I feel as though I'm walking on air!'

'I really am pleased for you, Emma,' Linda told her as the other two left the room. 'I could tell that you were crazy about Daniel the night of the dance and that he was just as smitten.'

'Really?' Emma shook her head in amazement. 'I had no idea, although Daniel seemed to think that I knew how he felt.'

'Well, I'm just glad that you had such a wonderful time. You deserved it, Emma, after all the rotten things that happened.' Linda paused. 'Did you hear that the police have found out who stole Paula's ring? The jeweller told Gary when he went to buy me this. Turns out it was Alison Banks—remember her?'

Emma frowned. 'Alison Banks…not the young girl whose husband was in the army!'

'That's right. Evidently, she overheard Paula telling you about the ring and took it on an impulse while Paula was having her scan.' Linda shrugged. 'I don't think she was thinking clearly at the time because she was so upset about her miscarriage. She told the police that she sold it and used the money to buy food and presents for Christmas. Her husband couldn't understand where all the stuff had come from and made her tell him what had happened. Then he took Alison to the police.'

'Oh, the poor girl! Grief does some very strange things to people. I do hope the police take that into account,' Emma said sadly.

'I'm sure they will.' Linda looked up as Daniel suddenly appeared. 'Oh, time I was on my way. Two's company and three's definitely one too many!'

Emma shook her head in despair as Linda left. 'She really is incorrigible!'

'I'd say that she showed a rare degree of sensitivity,' Daniel replied, coming into the staffroom and firmly closing the door behind him. He took Emma in his arms and kissed her thoroughly.

'That's better. I was starting to get withdrawal symptoms.'

Emma laughed. 'It's only ten minutes since you last saw me!'

'And that's far too long.' He kissed her again then sighed when his beeper began to trill. 'Why does that always have to happen at the most inopportune moments? Anyway, I'll see you later.'

One last kiss and he was gone, leaving Emma smiling. She seemed to be floating as she made her way to the ward, and the feeling didn't go away for the rest of the day. Daniel was waiting in the foyer for her when she finished work. Emma stepped from the lift and smiled as she saw him, her own walking, talking, *loving* Christmas present. Santa had really pulled out all the stops this year!

'Ready to go home?' he asked, taking hold of her hand. Emma knew that everyone in the hospital now knew that they were getting married, thanks to Linda and the grapevine. She saw a lot of looks being cast their way and smiled. She loved Daniel and he loved her—she wanted the whole world to know how they felt!

'More than ready. Let's go and collect Amy, shall we?'

They left the hospital and drove through the town. The lights were still on even though Christmas had been and gone. Soon it would be time to take down the decorations for another year.

Emma smiled as she looked at Daniel sitting beside her. This had been the best Christmas ever, and the best thing of all was that it was going to last for ever. They were going to be a *real* family all year round, not just for Christmas!

MILLS & BOON®

Makes any time special™

*Mills & Boon publish 29 new titles
every month. Select from...*

Modern Romance™   Tender Romance™

Sensual Romance™

Medical Romance™ Historical Romance™

MAT2

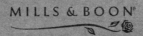

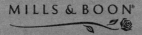

MILLS & BOON®

Medical Romance™

THE LOVING FACTOR by Leah Martyn

Dr Cate Clifford's new locum partner, Andrew Whittaker, was just the type of man she could fall in love with. Yet as their friendship deepened, she realised Andrew was not all that he seemed...

A LEAP IN THE DARK by Jean Evans

Life on the Island of Hellensey was just the way Dr Kate Dawson wanted until the arrival of Dr Sam Slater. Her divorce two years previously had shattered her trust in men but was Sam about to change that?

WORTH THE RISK by Sarah Morgan
New Author

Dr Ally McGuire and Dr Sean Nicholson were a formidable professional team. Neither was about to jeopardise their working relationship until, after one unexpected night of passion, Ally became pregnant...

On sale 5 January 2001

Available at most branches of WH Smith, Tesco, Martins, Borders, Easons, Volume One/James Thin and most good paperback bookshops

0012/03b

The perfect gift this Christmas from

MILLS & BOON®

*3 new romance novels &
a luxury bath collection*

for just £6.99

Featuring

Modern Romance™

The Mistress Contract
by Helen Brooks

Tender Romance™

The Stand-In Bride
by Lucy Gordon

Historical Romance™

The Unexpected Bride
by Elizabeth Rolls

FREE

4 BOOKS
AND A SURPRISE GIFT!

We would like to take this opportunity to thank you for reading this Mills & Boon® book by offering you the chance to take FOUR more specially selected titles from the Medical Romance™ series absolutely FREE! We're also making this offer to introduce you to the benefits of the Reader Service™ —

- ★ FREE home delivery
- ★ FREE monthly Newsletter
- ★ FREE gifts and competitions
- ★ Exclusive Reader Service discounts
- ★ Books available before they're in the shops

Accepting these FREE books and gift places you under no obligation to buy; you may cancel at any time, even after receiving your free shipment. Simply complete your details below and return the entire page to the address below. **You don't even need a stamp!**

YES! Please send me 4 free Medical Romance books and a surprise gift. I understand that unless you hear from me, I will receive 6 superb new titles every month for just £2.40 each, postage and packing free. I am under no obligation to purchase any books and may cancel my subscription at any time. The free books and gift will be mine to keep in any case.

M0ZEC

Ms/Mrs/Miss/Mr ....Initials ....
BLOCK CAPITALS PLEASE

Surname ....

Address ....

....

....Postcode ....

Send this whole page to:
UK: FREEPOST CN81, Croydon, CR9 3WZ
EIRE: PO Box 4546, Kilcock, County Kildare (stamp required)